DARK AND DEADLY THINGS

by

KELLY MARTIN

Dark and Deadly Things
by Kelly Martin

To the brave souls in the world,
and to those (like me) who peek between your fingers.

Molly Drake fell in the lake.
Tied to a stake.
The souls she did take.

Molly Drake was filled with dread.
Water covered her head.
Until she was dead.

Molly Drake, your wish come true.
A price for two.
She'll come for you.
— Children's Rhyme

CHAPTER ONE

IT IS A STRANGE FEELING IN life to watch your ghost hunter of a father live on TV while eating popcorn next to your dead mother.

That's not entirely true. It's a strange feeling to be sure, and my mother is most assuredly dead. But she isn't next to me. She's across the room, standing between the old mahogany grandfather clock that needs to be dusted and the old cabinet television that belonged to my grandma in the eighties. It doesn't work anymore, the television that is. Now the cabinet is used as a stand for the newer TV version, one that I don't have to get up and change the channels on.

My mother looks like television static. She's glitching, coming in and out of focus. Her white gown is splattered with dark, red blood. Her hair is black and soaking wet. If I didn't know better, and I do know better, I'd say there would be a puddle of water under her when she disappears. But there won't be. There never is. I hate to admit that I've looked before. Guess I'm a curious sort.

I don't know why my mother is in a white gown or why her hair is wet. The last time I saw her, she had on jeans and a black t-shirt. And I have no idea where the blood came from, and she can't tell me. Oh she moves her mouth like she's trying to communicate. She even screams at me sometimes, silent screams that break my heart and make me cover my eyes. I don't want to see her. I don't want to see any of them.

They never found my mom's body.

I think she's trying to tell me what happened to her, but I can't make it out. I'm sorry about that. I've even tried the Electronic Voice Phenomena machines I used to use on the hunts. Heck, I got an EVP app on my phone to try to understand her. Nothing works. I've told her that many times. I'm not sure she believes me. I'm not sure I believe myself.

I toss another popcorn kernel in my mouth and try my hardest to ignore her. She doesn't make it easy.

Voices from the television draw my attention.

"Is there anyone here with us?"

"God, Silas, these EMF readings are off the chart."

My mother glares in my father's direction on the screen.

She's not happy with him.

I can relate.

She glares in my direction.

She's not happy with me.

I can relate to that too.

"Yeah, huge spikes in this corner too. Think we should do a reading?" Silas asks like he doesn't know the answer. Like this isn't one big scam, with every word and every camera angle painstakingly mapped out. I know this because up until six months ago, I was right there with them. Beside my father, gathering *evidence* and kissing Silas in dark corners in the supposedly haunted house on the night vision camera.

It made the network happy.

Truth be told, it made me happy.

I truly thought Silas Ford loved me. I think he did at one time. I know I loved him.

Then Mom died.

Silas changed.

And I turned twenty-one.

After that, the world went to hell.

Mom has glitched next to the window. I can see the curtains blowing through her. This won't cause me to need therapy in the least. Somehow, I don't think any therapist worth his or her salt will believe me anyway.

The host, Stan, comes over to Silas and my dad, joining their EMF discussion. Stan reminds the viewers that we are live at Hale House, the sight of many violent hauntings. Mama and little girl Hale believe in the ghosts. The dad doesn't. College-aged son, Abel, doesn't either. He's in the living room with the rest of the family, watching the ghost hunt unfold on the live feed along with the folks tuning in.

The network has done a live Halloween event for the past five years. This is the one that means the most. Do or die. Canceled or renewed. I overheard my dad and Mr. Owens at the studio talking a few weeks before I quit. Ratings are way down, and they are having a dry ghost spell—a dry *real* ghost spell, that is. If they don't get better evidence quick, it'll be over with. No more *Dark and Deadly Things*.

Little does Mr. Owens know that my dad faked evidence way before that.

How do I know that?

How indeed.

My mom glitches again, and I throw another piece of popcorn in my mouth. I shouldn't be watching the show. I should be out with my friends getting drunk or, at the very least, watching something that isn't this. I don't know why I'm curious about it. I guess I want to give my dad the benefit of the doubt. Even though he's been faking ghost evidence for months, I want this time to be the real deal. Just once I want to think the best of him.

My mother's mouth moves, and her brows furrow.

I suppose it's bad to want real ghosts to be haunting the

Hale House. I mean, from what I've gathered from Stan, a bastard who can't keep his hands to himself, the little girl and the mom are pretty scared. The ghost, or whatever it is, has been knocking things around the house and slamming doors—typical things, in my experience. What makes this case unique is how adamantly the father is against it. Like he is living in complete denial. I'm rooting for the little girl. I know what it's like to see things and have no one believe you.

The show cuts to my dad and Silas walking into the living room with the mom, dad, sister, and brother Hale. The little girl, who can't be older than six, is huddled in her mom's lap. The mom looks equally scared. The dad... I think he'd rather be anywhere else. The son? He's... He looks about my age and is pretty to look at. Brown hair that is a bit too long. A five o'clock shadow. I can't tell what color his eyes are, but I can bet they are one thing... dreamy.

My mom glitches and is gone.

I'm sure she will turn up again sometime.

I don't mean to sound callous about my mom. I hate that she's dead. I hate it so much. I love my mom, and at first I loved having her around, even in ghost form. But there's nothing I can do for her. I can't help her. I don't know how she died, though I have an idea. Her body was never found.

I want to help her, and I can't. I want to make it better for her, and there's no way. How can you save something that is already dead? How can you fix it? No one believes me. Not even my dad, world famous Ghost chaser Roger Morgan, believes me... and he's paid to find ghosts.

"We haven't finished our investigation yet, but I wanted to sit you guys down and show you what we've found."

"You've found nothing," I mumble to the television as I slurp my drink. "Because you are a big fake!"

If there had been a ghost on television, I would have seen it. I don't know why or how or when it started, but I've always been cursed to see ghosts, which, I suppose, is handy for a ghost hunter. Only my dad never believed me, and when I found out he was faking evidence, well, no matter how well Silas Ford kissed, I was gone like the wind.

Of course, by that time, I don't think it mattered much to Silas either.

The family sits down at a large round table. The front door is to their back. The kitchen door is behind Silas and Roger. A hallway is to the family's left.

"I want you to take a listen to what we found," my dad says.

"Baby…" The EVP plays. *"Baby."*

"Baby!" The mom jumps up. "It's saying baby. Did you hear that, John?"

The father shakes his head. "Sounds like static to me."

Clearly not static to me and obviously not to the people watching. The show's live twitter feed, which is scrolling on the bottom as it airs, is going crazy. One lady even claimed to see a black figure in the hallway beside the Hale family. Good Lord. Everyone in this world has gone mad.

I suppose I have my father to thank for that. He used to catch real evidence. Now he manipulates millions of viewers.

The little girl is shaking.

My appetite is gone.

"That's not what I heard, Mommy." She's adamant about this. *"It doesn't say baby. It says her name. It says Molly. And it says it's going to kill you and me because you made her do it."*

"That's enough!" John Hale slams his fist into the table, hushing the little girl instantly. She buries her face in her mother's neck. *"Stop this. Stop all of it. You faked the recording. I know you did! I've been reading up on you."*

I sit up and put the bowl of popcorn on the table. Oh my… this might be getting good.

"I haven't. I've never…"

"Don't play stupid with me, Roger Morgan. I know all about you. Faking evidence when you can't find any."

"You invited me here." My dad sits up straighter, and his

eyes cut to the camera and back to John.

This is live television, people. My dad's livelihood is on the line. If this goes sour, he loses everything... everything that's important. He's already lost me.

"She invited you!" He points his finger accusingly at his wife whose face has turned the same color as my father's. *"She did! I think she's filling my daughter's imagination with nonsense!"*

My father puts his hands out as if to calm John Hale. *"Listen, I haven't faked anything..."*

Lie number one.

"That said, I have something else to show you... something we caught..."

The little girl shakes her mother's shoulders. Even from here, I can see the fear in her eyes. *"It doesn't say baby, Mommy. It says Molly. It says it's going to kill us because of you."*

The mother pulls the daughter close and rocks her gently. The mom looks terrified. I would too if some ghost called Molly said she was going to kill me.

The men aren't paying attention to them. Of course they aren't. My dad hasn't paid attention when any female speaks in months.

"If you just watch." My father motions toward the computer screen next to him on the table.

"I don't want to see it. Get out of my house." John Hale stands, as does my father.

Silas stays sitting, and he smirks at the camera.

"Sir, you do have ghosts here. I know you do! But I wanted to reassure you... reassure your wife and daughter that no matter what we caught on EVP, there's no reason to be afraid. I don't think it has any malicious intent."

John Hale's eyes grow to be the size of saucers. *"It said it was going to kill my wife and daughter, if you believe what Lindsey says! How much more malicious can you be?"*

"You said you didn't believe it." My dad, always the voice of reason.

"You little..."

While Mr. Hale and my dad get into a verbal fight, which I'm afraid will escalate into a physical one—not that the network would mind, they'd probably love the publicity—something on the TV screen catches my eye. It's behind the family, in the hallway coming from the bedrooms.

A black mass.

And it's coming fast.

No... no... no!

The hair on my arms stands up as I accidently kick the coffee table, knocking the bowl over and scattering popcorn to the floor. No. I've only ever seen something like that one time. I don't want to see it again. This one is moving so much faster than the last one!

I fumble in my pocket until I find my cellphone and call my dad. He needs to get the family out. Now! They can't go through what I went through!

I hear his phone ring on television, stopping his fight with John mid-insult. He pulls the phone from his pocket and looks at the name. Then my father looks straight into the camera, straight into me.

"Pick up the phone!" I scream.

My mom glitches in front of the television. She's yelling something at me, something I don't have time to understand. Without thinking, I sling the coffee table out of the way and slide through her until my nose is right on the television screen. "Answer your phone!"

The black mass glides through the doorway. "Dad!" I scream. "Answer the phone!" John Hale is still yelling at my father, but he is looking at the camera mounted toward the ceiling. Looking at me.

He taps it a few times and shakes his head, as he puts the phone back into his pocket.

"Dad, no!" I bang on the television harder. I end the call and fumble as I hit the redial button. He has to see it. He has to feel it.

I can feel the mass from here. Dark, violent, evil.

Sickening.

The mass stops right behind my father.

The little girl, Lindsey, points from the safety of her mother's lap.

Mary hugs Lindsey and grabs her son by the leg. "You're not getting them!" she screams.

The lights flicker.

Then the TV goes to static.

CHAPTER TWO

MY DAYS ARE MOSTLY SPENT TRYING to avoid the world. I don't get online much, and when I do, I instantly regret it. It has been a week since the live broadcast—since most of the Hale family died—and the stories haven't stopped yet. Maybe a million people, tops, watched the live event when it first aired. Now, over fifty million have watched the replay on YouTube. Many more have watched the remixes, the reaction videos, the analysis, and everyone has the same thing to say... my dad is a murderer.

The one good thing that came out of the situation is my dorm mate, Sadie, decided she'd had enough of this fiasco and put in a transfer to switch rooms. I never liked Sadie anyway; she always took my toothbrush when she thought I wasn't looking.

My room is on the first floor, and for the last few days, a gaggle of photographers have had their camera aimed directly at my window. I shoot them a bird every so often, just so they have something to publish. I'm a humanitarian that way.

I'm a bit of a celebrity in my own right, though I really, really hate to describe myself as that. I was on *Dark and Deadly*

Things for four years before it all went to hell, before I decided I didn't want to live in the lie anymore. Had we seen ghosts in those four years? Yes. Well, *I* had. My father had too in the earlier episodes. I take that back. I think he actually saw a ghost. He certainly claimed to feel them, hear them, feel cold spots, and see hits on the infrared camera. So yeah, he saw *evidence* of ghosts sometimes. However, it's one thing to hear an EVP; it's another to believe your daughter actually sees ghosts. That was too much for my dad, who I guess assumed that dragging me around looking for ghosts at such a young age had messed with my mind somehow.

I'm not the one who's insane.

Technically, my father is.

Roger Morgan was transferred directly to Sunnyside Mental Institution once he was cleared from the hospital. He'd gotten injured in the attack, which is a nice word for it, but he had been injured the least so that meant he must have caused it.

Because no one else saw the black mass behind him… no one except Looney Laura from Massachusetts, who came forward and talked to CNN about what she saw before the massacre. The evidence was on Twitter from that night. The *Dark and Deadly Things* live stream. She's been the source of many memes herself. Looney Laura has also become a celebrity in her own right, singing karaoke in a car on a late night talk show.

Fun times for all.

No one believed Looney Laura, of course. It reminded me of some of the footage of the O.J. Simpson trial I'd seen on the History Channel. The ex-host of *The Tonight Show*, Jay Leno, had made a bit of a spectacle about it. The Dancing Itos and all that. People laughed and laughed, totally forgetting that two people had died.

That's what this seems like. The jokes that have been made at Looney Laura's expense… at my Dad's expense… at my expense aren't funny. Not in the least, but people eat them up. Late night shows have had a field day. Imagine ghosts being real? Lunacy! And the internet has been even less kind. There is a meme of the Hale family with a red circle and a line through them. The caption reads: *Who ya gonna call? Not Roger Morgan.*

My dad was charged with five deaths: Gary, the soundman, who I'm still not sure they have found all of; Sebastian, the cameraman who had his eyes blown out; and then the family members, John Hale, Mary Hale, and Lindsey Hale. Lindsey was found covering her brother. The little six-year-old saved her twenty-something older brother. I don't know how that little thing did it. I don't know why. We may never know.

I'd love to watch the camera footage to see what the hell happened. I mean, I wouldn't *love* to watch it. I don't want to see it. But I think maybe if I saw it, I could hone in on the ghost or spirit or whatever. It doesn't act like a ghost. I've only ever seen one thing like it before, and it wasn't a pleasant experience.

Abel Hale, the only survivor of his family, is supposed to get out of the hospital today. I got online long enough to see that update. I figured as much since half the photographers had left my grassy knoll. Maybe if I wait them out long enough, they will all be gone, and I can move on with whatever life I have left.

My mother hasn't come back either.

When I turned around after the TV went to static on Halloween, she was gone. I haven't seen her since. I don't know what that means, but what I do know is that I miss her. I don't know what to do. How do I help my father? Is there any way to prove he's innocent? What about me? Call me Haley Joel Osment; I see dead people. That can't be normal.

More than anything, I want her to come back and be real, not be a ghost or an echo or whatever she is. I want her to be real and solid. I want her to be alive and hug me. Tell me everything will be all right. From where I'm sitting right now, nothing will be all right again. Nothing.

There is a knock on my door. Whoever it is can go away, find some other girl whose father was just accused of murder on live national television to sell her Girl Scout cookies too. I don't want any. I want a hole, and I want to crawl into it. Is that too much to ask?

"Elise?"

I jump from my bed and freeze, not really sure what to do. It can't be him. I don't want to talk to him... how did he get past the photographers?

"Elise, I know you're in there. You haven't left this room for days. Let me in. We need to talk."

Silas Ford. The other survivor of the attacks.

The one I used to love.

The only one I wouldn't have missed.

As I run my fingers through my oily hair, I realize I seriously need a shower, but you never know when someone will take a picture of you nowadays. I weigh the pros and cons. No matter how quiet I am or how much I really don't want to open that door, Silas won't leave. Knowing him and how vindictive he has become lately, I wouldn't be surprised if he hasn't handed out my dorm room key to every photographer outside just to spite me. Moron.

"Elise Morgan. Please. I need to talk to you. Now."

Well, when he puts it so nicely. I open the door, but only as far as the chain on top will allow. Take that, Silas Ford.

"Really? You aren't going to let me in?" Silas is tall, at least a foot taller than me, if not more. He has on a black shirt that hugs his muscles, which I'm sure is done on purpose to either intimidate me or turn me on. With Silas, I never knew which. His beard has grown out more since I saw him on television. He went from scruffy to having a full on man-beard. I kinda like it. I mean if it were on someone else. Not

Silas cause… no. Maybe Silas before he got all possessive, but not now.

"What do you want?" I wonder if I sound angry enough, because I'm going for angry.

"I came to check on you. Are you all right?"

Now what kind of stupid question is that?

"I'm peachy. Never better." I try to shut the door, but he puts his forearm in the way. When did he get so strong?

"I'm serious, Elise? Are you okay? Look, I know where they took your father. To lose him so soon after your mother…"

"Don't." I won't cry. I don't have it in me to cry right now. I think I've already used up all my tears. Even if I hadn't, if I had every tear still left in my eyes, I would be damned if I'd cry in front of Silas. "Don't you mention my mother. And don't come here pretending to care about me."

"I do—"

"Stop." I choke the word out. And here I thought I was so brave. "Just stop. Thank you for coming, but I need some time alone."

"And I get it. I do." He doesn't move his hand from the door. "I just wanted to see if you—"

"If I what?"

"If you saw… what happened?" Silas looks up at me from under his lashes like he doesn't want to come right out and ask, but he's dying to know the answer. He has two black eyes, black and blue and ugly. His eyes were beautiful compared to the side of his face. Looks like a baseball bat got a hold of him. Whatever happened at that house had done a number on him, which made sense if the police didn't think he had anything to do with it and my dad did. Dad didn't have one scratch. Not one.

"If I saw what happened?" There is no way I heard him right.

"Yeah, I mean if you saw the live stream. If you saw…

anything?" Silas. I'd told him about seeing ghosts one night when we were hunting, and it sort of came out. He laughed at first, and then when he realized I was serious, he let my hand go and gave me the strangest look. He told me I was crazy, in so many words. Said I didn't need to tell anyone else because they wouldn't believe me and would lock me up. That solidified my plan because if the one person I loved couldn't handle the fact that I see ghosts, how would someone I didn't know? I regret ever telling him now. He'll use it against me some day. I know it.

He crosses his arms and taps an impatient finger.

Oh good, we're having this conversation. "I saw the light flicker and then the static."

"Nothing else?"

Like I'd ever tell him. "Nothing else."

"Are you being honest with me?"

For the love of… "No, I'm lying through my teeth, Silas. What do you think?"

He stares at me for entirely too long. Long enough for me to notice his eyes. Not the bruises around his eyes, the cut on his lip, or even the stitches on his hairline, but his actual eyes. I used to love his eyes. They were a beautiful light blue. The color of the sky on a warm spring day. His eyes have darkened over time, turning from a bright blue to almost black.

"I think you didn't see anything."

Well, good. I'm not a half bad liar then. "Anything else?"

I shouldn't be so ill with him, not really. He's all bruised up on one side of his face like he was slammed against the wall. There is a burn on the side of his neck. One I can't see completely, and I can't fight the urge to pull his collar down and look. I almost act on that impulse because, why not, when reality and sanity—ha!—come back to me. I'm not touching him. He'd probably consider it a sign of forgiveness, and I most certainly haven't forgiven him. I'd rather die a slow, horrible death than ever think a nice thought about him.

Silas smirks.

I see nothing to smirk about.

"I'm sorry about your father," he says, surprising me.

"You're what?"

"I'm sorry about your father. I wish it hadn't ended that way. I wish it hadn't been him."

Red.

That's all I see.

I see red and feel anger, feel it bubbling up inside of me so fast and so hard that I can't make it stop. Silas must see it too because he takes a step back.

I'll.

Kill.

Him.

"You're sorry about my father?" I slam my hand against the door so hard Silas flinches. "You wish it hadn't ended the way it did?" I have to stop myself from unlocking the door. I'm shaking so hard and my emotions are so unpredictable at this moment that I don't trust myself. "Well, guess what? Me too! But do you know what else? My father didn't do what they said he did."

"Then who did? Or wait, even better knowing you, *what* did?" Silas challenges. Oh Glory. He's lucky I'm not opening this door.

"I have no idea. It could've been you for all I know." Not fair, but still.

He glares at me. "Why would I do such a thing?"

"Why would my father?"

"Elise, even you have to admit it looks bad. After what happened with your mother... your father was there that night too."

"So was I." So was I, and I wish to God I could forget it. "And so were you."

"Look, I know you don't want to think badly of your father, but I was there at the Hale House. I saw..."

"You saw nothing. It was pitch black when the lights went out. You. Saw. Nothing."

I slam the door in his face and bolt it shut. I slide down to the floor with my back to the door and expect a knock, a scream, a yell… something. Instead I'm greeted with silence.

Silas Ford can kiss my ass. My father didn't do this, but something inside that house did. It's evil and powerful, and it needs to be stopped.

Someone should stop it.

Someone other than me.

I put my head in my hands and rock. Someone other than me.

CHAPTER THREE

MARY HALE'S BODY HASN'T BEEN FOUND.

Just like my mom, there is blood—positively identified blood—but no body.

Still, life must go on, and going on means burial. John and Lindsey Hale are being laid to rest today. I don't want to go to the funeral. I mean, I do. I feel like I should. Then again, I might be the last person Abel Hale wants to see. After all, my father is accused of killing Abel's entire family. Not many ways to have a pleasant conversation with that hanging over our heads.

It has been two weeks since the incident. Incident, that sounds so generic, so sterile. So nice and clean and proper. From what I hear, there wasn't anything nice or clean or proper about the crime scene. The police came once and showed me pictures, asked me if there was anything I might know to help them understand the case. I took it to mean anything that could help them form a case against my father. No, I had nothing to help them do that—and since I doubted they want to hear about how I saw the big black mass in the room or how my father had faked evidence but didn't have to this time—then no, I had nothing to say.

They still showed me pictures. Lots and lots of pictures. I do wish I could've helped more, but there was nothing I could really tell them. I know one thing, though. I've got to figure out some way to prove my father didn't do it.

But how can you prove a ghost killed people?

I need a drink. It's five o'clock somewhere, even if it's only a little after noon here.

Southern Tennessee University frowns on drinking in your dorm. Southern Tennessee University can bite me. I'm an adult. I'm twenty-one, and if I want to drink a damn bottle of whiskey in one sitting, then it's my God-given right. As long as no one knows...

I'm a good girl in rebel's clothes.

I kill two shots of whiskey before I decide maybe I've had enough. Filled with liquid courage, I go to the window and look outside. Most of the photographers have gone. Most assuredly to the Hale funeral. That means I should stay here. Or, hey, use the break to go to the grocery store. There is only so much tuna fish a girl can eat. And I'm out of crackers. And I haven't left this room in twelve days, not even for classes. Thank the Lord my professors are allowing me to complete my semester online.

It might be time to get some fresh air. I hope people don't find it offensive if I pick today to come out into the world again—albeit undercover. People are offended easily nowadays, and truthfully I don't want to hear it. I don't know why I'm being treated like the criminal. I wasn't even at the house. I had nothing to do with it. My father didn't either. I wish I could prove it.

Knowing that the world will find something to be offended by no matter what I decide to do, I grab a towel and head toward the shower. It's been forever. I need a good hosing off. I wash my hair, and for the first time in two weeks, I take time to style it. My hair is dark brown, like my mother's;

only unlike hers, mine is way down below my shoulder blades. My mom's was right below her collarbone. Thanks to a rebellious streak after I left *Dark and Deadly Things,* I cut off thick bangs. Now I'm at that in-between stage of cutting them or letting them grow out. They are so close to falling into my eyes. I should pin them back, but for some reason, hiding behind my hair sounds like a good idea. I pull half my hair up into a barrette and let the rest hang over my shoulders.

I have to admit it feels good to be clean. Such a weird thing to take for granted. Instead of basic funeral black, I put on a white day dress with the express purpose of not going to the graveyard. I figure, if I put this on, there is no way I'll go to the cemetery no matter how much I try to talk myself into it.

I put on a light pink lipstick, add color to my cheeks, and throw on some white sandals. Even though it's the middle of November, Tennessee has decided to be all weird and not have a fall. It's in the low eighties today. Normally I would've loved it. I've never been one to like cold weather much. Too bad the warm weather is wasted on the year when I stay holed up in my room for weeks on end. Thank the Lord for online classes (and understanding professors) or I'd have failed out already.

I pass a few girls in the hallway on the way back to my room. None speak. Some gawk. Good for them. Gawk away. This could be them someday. It isn't like I chose this weird life. A naked girl walks past, and her eyes catch mine. I have to force myself to keep moving. I can't deal with this today.

When I get to my door, I feel eyes on me, so I do what every responsible girl does… I opened my door so freakin' fast and lock it shut behind me.

Like a locked door could keep a ghost away.

When I turn around, Naked Girl is standing in front of me, glitching and staticing away.

Her lips are moving, and her hands are wildly animated for someone who is naked. This girl doesn't care if she's seen naked in front of God and everybody.

"I don't understand what you're saying."

Her face falls. I guess she feels like this is her one chance to get her voice heard, and she has lost it.

"I'm sorry." But it's too late. She's already glitched out, leaving me alone.

I hate that I'm getting used to this, the seeing ghosts, feeling them, knowing that there isn't anything I can do to help them.

I refuse to go to the graveyard today. Good thing I'm not.

Not only am I wearing the forbidden color, but I also see ghosts and cemeteries are full of them. We used to drive by them, and seeing the ghosts looking around, lost, would break my heart. In my opinion, cemetery ghosts are the saddest of all. They don't have any real purpose in the world. A lot of ghosts seem to stay close to home or to a loved one. Cemetery ghosts are just... there. Like they missed their light, like they should have gone on and didn't... and they know it. Or they are afraid to go on. Maybe they are at the cemetery trying to connect with their body. That... is an unpleasant thought.

In any case, I wish I could help them — except for reuniting them with their rotting corpse... because no.

This power, this gift, is a total curse if I can't help these lost souls move on.

If I can't help my mom move on.

She's dead. I know that. I hate it, and I wish it weren't true. But I also hate the feeling that she's hurting, that there's nothing I can do to save her or get her out of the loop she's in, if that's what's happening to her.

I grab my purse, plaster a solemn smile on my face, and head out the door. I can't be too happy or too sad at this moment. People are watching and people talk... they always do.

I won't go to the cemetery.

I *will* go to the grocery store.

I'll buy some food.

I'll get fresh air.

If anyone finds me, I'll answer their questions appropriately, and I'll be the best Elise Morgan I can be. If I see any ghosts, I'll ignore them because… who wouldn't?

I walk down the hallway with my head held high.

I'm not going to the cemetery.

The naked girl has her hands out for me.

CHAPTER FOUR

I AM A MORON.

A complete and utter moron.

Walk to the store, Elise.

Get some food, Elise.

Out and back, Elise. Don't linger too long because someone will see you and snap your picture, Elise. Everyone has a damn phone with a damn camera on it. Those people all think they're professional photographers. Posting pictures on Instagram like they are the next coming of abandoned-house photography.

On their cellphones…

And they love to have the next viral video… and what would be more viral at the moment than Elise Morgan out and about while the entire Hale family, sans Abel, is being buried. I knew better than to leave the dorm.

And here I am.

Like an idiot.

And not just any idiot…

No, I'm the idiot at the cemetery at the freakin' Hale funeral!

I swore I wouldn't come. I'm in my white dress for God's sake. But something led me here. I'm not exaggerating. I was walking, not really thinking about anything, when something caught my eye.

A ghost, of course. I think it's all I see sometimes. She wore a white gown just like my mom. Not all ghosts wear white gowns like my mom does or the ones in horror movies. In my experience, ghosts wear what they died in, hence why Naked Girl is naked. Poor Naked Girl. I can't imagine being like that, naked and afraid for all eternity.

But none of that is really important. What is important is that I saw the ghost lady in a white gown standing at the gate of the cemetery, as lots of ghosts do. Her gown is long. Her hair is long, brown, and wet.

At first, I think it's my mother.

I'm wrong.

But I do recognize the woman.

I wish to God I didn't.

Mary Hale.

In all her afterlife glory.

She was watching her own funeral, watching as the bodies of her husband and her daughter were laid to rest in the warm November ground. Watched as her son Abel sat stone-faced, his eyes following the caskets down into the ground until they could no longer be seen.

She watched them.

I watched her.

I wanted to cry for her. Help her.

I couldn't do either.

So I did the only thing I could do. I stood next to her, giving her the only comfort I could, not being alone.

I hope she doesn't recognize me. If she knew I was Roger Morgan's daughter, the one who supposedly killed her, then it might get ugly. In my time, I've seen some ghosts get downright horrifying. If there is enough anger and force behind them, they can become violent.

Personally, I don't want violence right now. Or anytime. I want to help poor Mrs. Hale as best I can. If I only knew what that meant.

I can't help my mother. What makes me think I can help Mary? I guess, truth be told, it would be easier to help Mary. I don't know her, so I don't have that nagging feeling that her death is my fault. My mother's, yes. But not Mary… at least I don't think so. Yeah, I saw the big black mass, but I tried to call. I tried to make it all right. I tried…

Story of my life: I tried.

They should put that on my headstone.

Elise Morgan: the girl who tried.

There are lots of photographers around the other side of the cemetery at the gate. I'm sure they bombarded Abel as he went in, and they'll bombard Abel as he leaves. Vultures can't leave anyone alone.

I recognize a few of them. Derek the Dick is leaning against a red Mustang parked outside the gate, eating what I think is a donut. When my mother disappeared, he was the one who hounded me the most. Glad to see some things never change.

I wouldn't mind seeing him as a ghost someday.

Mary finally notices me. She blinks a few times and smiles when she seems to notice that I can see her. Then, like all the other ghosts, her mouth starts moving. She's clearly hoping I can hear her. I can't. It's part of my curse.

I tell Mary that, and her face falls. Why does this have to be so hard?

Because it's death, I suppose. Death isn't easy, though some call it the easy way out. A soul is a soul, whether living or dead. Only if they are dead, they can't exactly change the course of their lives.

Abel stands and walks over to the graves as his dad and sister are being lowered into the ground. No one should ever be in a casket as little as his sister's. They shouldn't ever be made. Such little things, such massive sadness. An entire life in one small, white box. I don't see her or her father here. They must have gone on to the other side, wherever that is. I don't know what makes a ghost stay behind. Maybe if I did, I could help them move on.

I don't think Mary wants to move on.

She's the only one without a casket because there is no body.

Just like my mother.

No closure.

No answers.

The wind blows, and a few dark clouds begin rolling in from the west. A storm is coming. I suppose it's poetic.

Orange, red, and yellow leaves dance around the cemetery like children at playtime, without a care in the world. When the wind stops, the leaves fall, and someone crushes them under their shoe.

I start to turn away when Abel's gaze catches mine. Even from this distance, I can see him glare at me, stare at me. I know I shouldn't be here. I wish I wasn't. Because he looked in my direction, Derek the Dick did too. And then all the others followed.

Lemmings. They're all lemmings.

They run toward me like I'm on fire and they want to catch it all on camera. The funeral attendees stand to see what all the commotion is about. Of course, it's all about me.

The photographers run.

The family runs.

I run.

Mary disappears.

I run as hard as I can, even though my shoes are too small and I haven't been able to go to the grocery store yet. I had a plan, damn it, and I screwed it up.

A few of the photographers have gotten smart and

hopped in their cars to chase me down. I'm on foot. This isn't a fair race.

My dorm isn't too far away, maybe three miles from the cemetery. It's the longest three miles of my life. I'm not what you'd call in shape, and running has never been my favorite thing. By the time I run past Pa Milton's Store and up through the trees on the Southern Tennessee University quad, my legs feel like they're going to give out. My legs, my lungs, my heart. Everything. I'm about to be as dead as all those other ghosts, and my forever outfit will be a white dress and shoes that don't fit.

This should not be something I'm worried about right now.

More important things and all that.

The sight of a girl running through the campus catches the attention of some of the other folks, who drag out their cameras and start either filming or snapping my picture. Doesn't matter. I can't run fast enough. I can't hide. There will be some picture of me running through the quad on the evening news.

Until there's some other disaster in this stupid small southern town, the focus won't be off me anytime soon.

I don't see that happening.

Derek the Dick is waiting for me outside my dormitory. "Why were you at the Hale funeral? Guilt?" He snaps away, grinning from ear to ear.

"So, how does it feel to have a serial killer as a father? How did he do it anyway? Did he do the same thing to your mother? Hack her up into little pieces so the police could never find her?"

You can talk about me.

You can talk about my father.

But you can never talk about my mother.

Derek the Dick promptly doubles over, his hands grab what I assume is a very small package, and I'm sure he could sing soprano in *The Phantom of the Opera* right about now. Strange how my knee just suddenly rose up and hit him in the junk like that. Hmmmm...

I stomp on his camera too as I stroll by him and, with my head held high, walk into my dorm, right past Naked Girl and all the way to my room. I lock every one of the seventeen locks I have installed on my door and fall face first on my bed.

I wish I could disappear like those ghosts, disappear and never come back.

Maybe start a new life somewhere... maybe not start a life at all.

If I could be anywhere but here, that would be great.

Naked Girl, who is glitching next to my dresser, frowns at me and crosses her arms. I don't think she approves. She can lump it.

Going out today was a stupid idea. I should've stayed in until everything died down, no pun intended. I knew better, and I did it anyway. I need a keeper. Or at least a handler. As it is, I'm an orphan with no siblings and no idea how to navigate the world. My college is paid for thanks to royalties from my time on *Dark and Deadly Things*. Thank the Lord for small favors...

But everything else, I have no idea.

For the first time, the real first time, it sinks in how alone I really am. No, I'm not technically an orphan. My father is alive, and I should focus on that. But in his situation, in the mental state he's in... I don't know. Maybe there are things worse than death.

If my dad never comes out of this, then that's it. I said before that I'd already cut myself off from my father thanks to the bogus TV evidence, but that's different. That was my choice. I always knew I could fix it if I wanted. I could call him whenever, and he'd answer like nothing had ever happened. We'd never had a big fight.

Now... now things are different.

There's a big difference when it is your idea to never see someone again and when it isn't.

I don't like this at all.

I want my mommy. I wish I could will her to show up. Instead, I'm stuck with Naked Girl, who I'd love to give a towel or some clothes... maybe figure out why she keeps silently screaming.

"You know I can't understand you, right?" I sound so tired.

She closes her mouth, and blood oozes from the corner of her lips.

"Do you have a name?"

She tilts her head like that's the stupidest question ever. She's not wrong.

"What *is* your name? Can you sign it?"

Naked Girl shakes her head and moves her mouth like she's hoping I'll read her lips.

I'm getting nothing.

"I'm sorry," I say. My heart can't take much more of this. I want to help these souls, I do. But how can I help them when I can't even help myself? How can I be the one to solve their problems when I can't even hear a word they say?

She blinks a few times, and her gaze falls to the floor, crushing whatever is left of my heart. There has to be a way to help these souls. There has to be.

"Are you in pain?"

Once the words are out of my mouth, I wish I could take them back. I don't want to know. If she's in pain, then my mother is in pain... Mrs. Hale is in pain. I can't... I don't want to think about that.

But once the question is out there, there's no way to take it away. Life doesn't come with a rewind button, though I so wish it did.

Naked Girl points to the gash on her neck and the knot on her forehead.

"They hurt?"
She nods.

CHAPTER FIVE

NAKED GIRL AND I BOTH JUMP when there's a knock on my door. She looks at me. I look at her.

If it's Derek the Dick, I swear to God, I'll kick him all over again. It isn't like he doesn't deserve it.

I don't have time to process the fact that Naked Girl is in pain, that it's possible that all ghosts are in pain… my mother among them.

There's pounding on my door again, frantic, quick. I'm not answering it.

I hate to tell whoever is on the other side, but I ain't going to be the one opening this door today.

And who in the world let them into the building anyway? You have to have a special code to get in the dorm, or someone has to buzz you in. Surely, one of the oh-so-sweet people in this dorm didn't let someone in to see me.

Sigh. I hate this place.

Naked Girl holds up one finger like she's telling me to wait. She glitches out and back before I can blink.

There's more knocking.

Naked Girl holds up her finger again. This time like she

wants to play charades.

Oh.

For.

The.

Love.

Of…

"One word… man? Is it a man?" Naked Girl nods. "Okay, it's a man. Does he have a camera? Cause if he does… no? No camera. Okay, he has longish hair. Beard? Does he have a beard? He does. Is it Silas?"

She shakes her head. She must have seen Silas when he visited me before.

"Then who is it?"

She smiles and winks at me. A dead girl winking at you while her soaked hair falls in her face is a very surreal experience. I can't say I like it. I do, however, like the fact that Naked Girl is helping me. It's nice to have a friend, even if my one friend is a naked ghost. Should make sleepovers fun.

"Miss Morgan?" Well it's a guy's voice. I'm pretty sure I've heard it before, but I can't place it. "I need to talk to you."

"I don't want to talk to you." I hope I sound as bitter as I am. I don't have the time or the desire to talk to anyone right now, especially not someone who'll probably just snap my picture and high tail it out of here when he gets what he wants.

"Miss Morgan, I'm Abel Hale. I need to talk to you."

My entire body freezes.

Abel Hale.

Is in my dorm.

Knocking on my door.

And he wants to talk to me.

Naked Girl gives me the I'm-so-sorry-but-that's-how-the-cookie-crumbles face. I'll remember that when it comes time to buy her a birthday present.

And here I thought she was my friend.

I go over to the door and rest my hand on the knob. I don't want to open it. I can't be face to face with Abel. I can't. I'm sure he blames my father for everything. Or Abel wants answers or something else I can't give him.

I can't move my hand away from the knob. And I can't turn it. It's like I'm stuck here somewhere between two choices, neither of them the right one.

The locks start to unlock one by one, definitely not by me, and the handle starts to shake.

I look to my right, and sure enough, there is Naked Girl turning the knob in all her glory. This is new. I'd heard about ghosts being able to move things, but I'd never seen it. Naked Girl has learned all about this how-to-be-a-ghost thing pretty fast. Doesn't mean I want to talk to Abel Hale though.

"Stop it," I whisper in my scariest voice.

Naked Girl ignores me and keeps right on turning.

"Stop!" My whisper turns into a growl. That's enough. She needs to stop. We're not friends, and there's no way she's making decisions for me.

No.

Just as I think those very empowering words, the door opens. There, in all his glory, is Abel Hale.

If Naked Girl weren't already dead, I'd kill her myself.

I glare in her general direction, and she disappears

Son of a...

Abel Hale, I do believe, has seen better days. Course, we'd all look like him if we'd buried our family not ten minutes ago. His hair is touching the collar of his white shirt. He has on a black tie, a clip on. I bet he has no idea how to tie a tie, and his father died before he could show his son properly.

Abel is taller than he looks on television. Dare I say, he's taller than Silas by a good half a foot. Like an afterthought, Abel has his black suit jacket folded in the crook of his arm. It's a very warm November. His muscles are threatening to bust out of his shirt sleeves. His jaw is hard and set. But it's his eyes that catch my attention the most.

This isn't a love story. I don't look into his eyes and automatically swoon. Under any other circumstance, I'm sure I could've swooned. His eyes are beautiful. A light green, the color of the spring sky before a storm. Beyond the color, I see the pain. The anguish of being in the same room as your parents and your sister when they're murdered. Of being in the same room when your mother disappears and is most likely dead.

I've been there.

If there's anyone on this whole entire planet who knows what he's going through, it's me.

If there's anyone on this whole entire planet he doesn't need to talk to right now, it's also me. There are girls starting to form a crowd outside. Their phones are at the ready. Abel doesn't deserve to be the object of their stupid social media obsessions. He deserves so much more.

It isn't that I want to invite him in. I do. I mean, I don't. There's nothing I can do for him. It isn't like I can answer any questions for him, and I sure as heck am not going to tell him about his mother's ghost at the funeral. There are some things that are better left not known. This is one of them.

But…

I also can't leave him outside with those photo-hungry girls around. Not to mention the photographers outside. So, I do what any self-respecting girl would do, I pull him into my room and lock the seventeen locks behind him.

After I finish my task and turn around, Abel is looking at me like I'm insane. Well, maybe the apple doesn't fall far from the tree. I take a deep breath, my mind racing with all the things I should and shouldn't say. What is the etiquette for this? What would Martha Stewart do?

"Uh… I'd ask you if you'd like something to drink, but I don't have anything."

Because everyone wants a Sprite after their family is

slaughtered. Smart, Elise. Very smart. I got rid of the whiskey. Dropped it in the trashcan outside the room on my way to the cemetery. Too much temptation there.

Wish I had it now.

"No, thank you, though." He wrings his hands like he's super nervous. That makes two of us. I wonder if he'll do small talk or cut to the chase.

I clear my throat. "Look, I'm sorry…"

"I saw you at the funeral."

So, no small talk for us.

I can feel my cheeks burn red. This dorm is so small, and now the walls are closing in on me more. I want out. I don't want to talk to him. I want a normal life. And I sure as hell don't want Naked Girl sitting on my bed watching all of this unfold. I tell her that with my eyes.

Abel looks toward the bed and then back to me. "You okay?"

"I should be asking *you* that." I laugh shyly. I've never been shy around guys before—well, not really. And I'm not shy now because Abel is hot. It's more than that. Much, much more.

Abel shrugs and slides his hands into his pockets. "I'm not fine. How can you be fine after that?"

"I was wondering the same thing." I motion for him to sit in my computer chair at the desk, which he does. I sit down on Sadie's old bed because Naked Girl has mine occupied. I hope this doesn't become a habit.

"I'm sorry about coming to the cemetery." I most sincerely am.

"Why did you come anyway?"

I shrug. There's no good answer, and most definitely not one he'll believe. It isn't like I can tell him I showed up because I saw the ghost of his mother standing at the gates. "I don't know. I didn't mean to. The photographers who are normally camped out here left, so I thought I would to. Get some fresh air."

"It gets stifling in here?"

"It does. But it's also my sanctuary, especially since my roommate moved out."

"Why'd she do that?"

I raise a brow at him.

"Ah." He smiles ever so gently, revealing a tiny dimple on his cheek. "Couldn't deal with the constant media attention."

"No." I'm as certain about that as I am of anything in the world.

"No?"

"She couldn't deal with me."

That got his attention in a way I didn't expect. I'm fairly sure if Naked Girl could eat popcorn, she'd be chugging it down by the way she's gawking at us. I guess she doesn't get much entertainment being dead and all.

"There's someone here with us," he says, most certainly catching my attention. Naked Girl sits up a bit straighter too.

"I think we'd know. It isn't a big room." Rule the first when dealing with the son of a family your father is accused of slaughtering: don't tell them there's a ghost in the room with you. He might use it to his advantage. Actually, he could be working for the police or the photographers, wearing a wire or something to try to get me to say something I'll regret and find more evidence against my father.

It sounds paranoid to me, too, but nowadays I never know what people will do.

"Please don't lie to me. I've had enough people lie to me these last two weeks to last me a lifetime." He sits up straighter in his chair. He has a look that's half puppy dog eyes and half dangerous. I'm not sure which one will win out. I hope puppy dog, but how can one say no to a puppy?

"I don't know what you're talking about." Another lie. Our relationship so far, and no I don't think we have or will ever have a real relationship, is quickly building on one lie after another.

"Elise." He clears his throat. "Look, I don't know what happened at my house two weeks ago. I have no idea, and I was in the room. I mean, you tell me how my sister saved me, my six-year-old sister, mind you. I was knocked out. I don't remember much. Not after the lights went out. My mom grabbed me. My sister screamed. The lights went out and so did mine. But I'm not an idiot. I know something happened, something…" His voice trails off.

"Something what?"

He averts his eyes for a second. I don't know if he's trying to find the right word, or if he knows the right word and just doesn't want to say it because he'll sound crazy.

"Abel?" I slide closer to him, fighting the urge to put my hand on his knee. "Something what?"

"She died for me," he says, his voice low, breaking my heart.

"We don't know that."

He doesn't seem to hear me. "She died for me. My mom disappeared for me. The police aren't looking for her because they say she's dead. And I…" He closes his eyes and takes a deep breath. "I don't know what to believe. I know something was in there. Something took my family, but I have to believe that my mom is alive. I have to. It makes no sense. Why would something leave some bodies, leave me alive, but take my mom if she was dead? It just… nothing adds up."

My chest is heavy. I know where his mom is. I saw her. She looked like my mom. I can't tell him that, though, because I feel like the only thing he's hanging on to is hope. I can't take that from him.

"What do you mean something?" I ask to keep him on track and hopefully stop thinking about his mother. Yeah, like that'll do any good. Like I've stopped thinking about my mother this entire time.

"Something…" He sighs. "Something supernatural."

I sit up straighter. "Something supernatural."

"I know how it sounds." He gets up and paces the five tiny steps he can take in my room.

I try to stop him and tell him I understand and believe him. He doesn't give me time. "Look, I need… I need to talk to your father."

At least that changed the subject. "That might be a problem. It would be easier to have a conversation with a vegetable right now than my father in the state he's in."

"You've seen him?"

I nod. "Once. A few days after the…" I cannot say incident around Abel. It was so much more than an incident to him.

"Yeah. I just need you to get me in to see him. That's all." Those big ole puppy dog eyes again. There's something about a grown man, he has to be twenty-one or twenty-two, when they give that look. The one people know they shouldn't listen to, but they do anyway.

He's laying it on thick right now.

"How do I know you don't want me to take you to my father so you can kill him?" A valid question.

His eyes narrow. "Why would you think I'd kill him? What kind of person do I look like?"

"The grieving kind." If I'm being honest. "And, truth be told, I don't know you from Adam. I don't know what you would and wouldn't do to my father, and frankly I don't want to find out."

I stand to show him the way out. I've been nice as long as I can. It's time for him to leave, for me to draw the curtains and lie on my bed in blessed solitude. I think I've earned it today.

Gold star for Elise.

Abel isn't getting the hint.

He plops back down in my computer chair and drapes his

arms over his knees like he has the weight of the world on his shoulders. I'm sure he does, or at least it probably feels that way to him.

"Look, Elise. I don't know what happened to my family in there. I was there, but I..." He looks down and seems to suddenly find his fingertips very fascinating. "I know that I have to find answers. I have to find the truth. Not what the police say. Not what the network says..."

"The network has talked to you?" That certainly gets my attention. The network hasn't called me once since it happened. Guess they don't want it to look like they're conversing with the murderer's daughter. Yes, the network honchos are just moral and highly esteemed folks. (They show *MonsterShark* fifteen times a day...)

"A few times. They wanted to give me their condolences."

I think he's half a second away from rolling his eyes. I can relate. Dealing with the network has never been a fun experience. When my dad first came up with the idea for *Dark and Deadly Things*, it was fun—exciting even. I've learned a lot since then.

"And ask you not to sue, I'm sure." I scoff. The producers and I aren't on the best terms. In fact, I dare say, I hate them almost as much as their new poster child Silas.

"Something like that." He smiles sadly. "Anyway, I can't get that night out of my mind."

"It's understandable since your family—"

He stands and cuts me off. "No, it's not just that!"

Naked Girl shrinks back into the shadows on my bed. I wish I could join her. Abel seems to see that his outburst scared me a bit. "It's... Something doesn't add up. A lot of things actually. I need to talk to your father. See if he can fill in the missing pieces."

"I wish I could help you." Truer words have never been spoken. "I truly do. But my father... he's not all there, if you know what I mean. He's not coherent, and when he is, it's my understanding that he sits in a corner and screams. He's been hurting himself, so they are keeping him restrained. I don't think he'll be able to tell you anything, and if he could, I wouldn't be one hundred percent convinced that it's accurate."

I hate to burst Abel's bubble, but it is what it is. My father can't help anyone. He can't even help himself. He keeps babbling about things that make no sense. He fights the nurses, fights the restraints, fights the drugs they give him to calm down. The media tells the folks that he's snapped. That it had been building for a long time until it just... boom.

I don't believe that for a second.

"I need to know where my mother is," Abel says out of the blue. I hadn't been expecting that.

"I thought the police found her blood." I try to act as dumb as I can. Which isn't hard.

"They did, but they also didn't find her body. Tell me, doesn't that seem a bit odd to you. Didn't the same thing happen to your mother?"

I feel my stomach turn as the image of my mother, cold, wet, alone, pops in my mind. I need a drink. I'd kill for some whiskey or wine or even champagne. We could toast to how screwed up my family is... what's left of us.

"I'm sorry." He backtracks. I assume he saw my facial expression—a cross between an excited otter and a scared baboon. "I'm... I'm sure you don't want to talk about your mother's death right now. God, it's only been, what six months?"

I nod. "Six long months."

"Does it get better?"

He sounds so sad, so lost. He's alone now, just like me. It isn't easy for either of us. I think maybe for one brief split second that we could help each other. Maybe if we could lean on each other, talk to each other, then maybe neither of us would really be so alone. We'd lived through similar experiences, but then again, he'd lived through his family being attacked. I'd only watched it from home—even though it had happened to me six months ago.

The thought of my poltergeist support group starts to fade away. He'd never agree to be in a group with me. Never.

"Elise?" he says when I don't answer right away. I have trouble listening with my thoughts screaming at me sometimes.

"Does it get better?" I sigh. No... no it doesn't, but what do I tell Abel? Should I give him hope, or should I give him reality? I wish there were a guidebook for this. I should write one. "I don't know if it gets better, but eventually it changes. It doesn't hurt as much, and you can function through your day. You might even go a second without thinking about it happening."

"I doubt it." He scoffs. If he doesn't stop rubbing his hands, they're going to blister.

"Yeah, me too."

He shakes his head like he's fighting off all the questions that are keeping him from asking the one big thing he's curious about. "When can we go see your father?"

There is no *please* or *Miss Morgan*.

Just "can we go see your father?" and nothing else.

Have we not had this conversation?

"I already told you. He hasn't been having very good days, though he does have a coherent moment every so often—or so the nurses tell me."

"Please, Elise. Even if it's a dead end and he has nothing for me or even remembers my mother, it'll make me feel better knowing I tried."

I don't see that I have a choice, but at least he did say please. There's so much pain in him. Pain and anger, sadness and frustration. I want to fix it. I want to help him. I can't help the ghosts, our mothers are proof of that, but I can try my very best to make Abel's life better.

"I'll take you, but you have to promise me one thing."

"Anything." He's smiling from ear to ear. He wouldn't be smiling if he saw how much of a bad idea this trip to see my father is.

"Whatever you do, don't mention my mother to my father. It might agitate him."

"Done. Anything else I should remember?" Abel is taking mental notes. He should be taking some on legal pads.

"Yes, there is." I grab my purse and start to head back out into the wild blue yonder. "This is the one and only favor you're getting from me. Once this is over, you don't hound me or come near me again. Got it?"

There isn't a hesitation in his voice. "Got it. Once this is over, and I talk to your father, I'll never bother you again. You won't see me. I promise."

Why does that make me feel so sad?

CHAPTER SIX

WE MAKE IT OUT OF MY dorm relatively easy. It only takes three twists, seven turns, one maneuver, and seventy dollars to one of the security guards to block the door as we get away. I don't like feeling like a fugitive. I don't like not being able to walk from my room anytime I want or, oh I don't know, live, without someone breathing down my neck with a camera. It'll only last for a few more days, tops. When something more interesting comes up, I know in my heart of hearts the folks with the cameras will leave Abel and me alone.

I just wish that would happen soon.

How sad is it to wish for a disaster for my own personal gain?

Oh well, I never claimed to be a saint. Quite the opposite actually.

Abel and I hop in different vehicles. It wasn't intentional on my part. I thought he was right behind me, and then bam, he wasn't. I saw him getting in a red Mustang down the road. Well then, isn't that the least conspicuous car in the world? I bet it's the same one Derek the Dick was leaning on at the funeral. I hope Abel disinfects it.

"Follow that red Mustang," I tell my driver, who turns around and looks at me like I'm crazy.

"We're going to the same place." It doesn't even sound like a convincing excuse to me, even though it's actually one hundred percent true.

"Uh huh." He grumbles and drives away. I'm sure he thinks we're some love spat gone wrong, or maybe he thinks I'm a jilted lover trying to get dirt on her boyfriend by trailing him. Truth be told, I don't care what he thinks. I wish I didn't care what anyone thinks. I mean, I'm twenty-one years old. I take care of myself. I pay my own bills, make my own money—well, I live off royalty payments, but still, I worked for that money. I'm my own woman.

Except when it comes to what people think about me, and then I'm a big pile of mush.

If I could change one thing about myself, that would be it. That and the stupid seeing-ghosts thing. That is unnecessary.

We pass the cemetery in our travels. Abel's mom is standing in the exact same place I left her. Through her static, I can see her arms are crossed, and she's looking into the cemetery. I wonder what she's thinking. I bet I don't want to know. I know I don't want to know.

My heart aches to tell Abel about his mom. I bet he's going into this with the hope that his mom is alive somewhere. It's probably why he came to me in the first place. I bet there's a little shred of hope that something will lead him to his mother. They never found a body after all, and that means, at least to him, that there's hope.

Hope is an evil thing.

I should tell Abel the truth before that hope destroys him like it does so many people in this world. I should, but I don't know if I can.

This hope, this finding his mom, might be the only reason he needs me. As much as I don't want him to, I think I need him as much as he claims to need me.

I need him because I think he knows there's more to the story. He was there in the room, and no matter what he says, he has to know more than he's letting on. Lord knows I do about the day my mother died.

And to top it off, Abel said—and I guess I was supposed to forget it because he acted like he didn't say it—he felt what was in the house. What does that even mean?

Taking him to see my father is probably the dumbest thing I've ever done.

My cab driver pulls up a few yards behind Abel. "In case you don't want him to see you," the helpful idiot, with a gap between his teeth so big I could drive a car through it, says. I know he thinks this is some sort of an underhanded deal.

"Thanks." I toss him a twenty and don't wait for the change. Maybe that's this guy's deal. Maybe he insults his passengers so much that they just want out of his cab quickly and don't wait for money back. If that's his deal, it's genius!

If it isn't, it needs to be.

Maybe that should be my new job. A cranky Uber driver who's so annoying patrons throw me money to get away from me. It could totally work.

Abel is waiting for me outside his car. The cab drives by, and because I'm such a nice upstanding citizen, I flip the driver a bird as he leaves.

I'm pretty sure that shocks the heck out of Abel because he laughs. Like, actually laughs. The man is standing in the same clothes he buried his family in, about to go inside and see the man who is charged with doing it, and he's laughing.

And here I thought I had issues.

"You okay?" I don't think he's okay.

Abel wipes the tears from his eyes. The man laughed harder than I thought. "Yeah, I mean, not really, but thanks."

"For what?" I'm pretty sure there's nothing in this world that would require him thanking me.

"For taking my mind off all this. For being, I don't know,

you."

He walks in front of me toward the hospital, and I just have to stand and gawk at the man. No one has ever thanked me for being me. Ever. I don't know why they would or why they would even think of it. I've always been the odd ball. I see dead people. Hollywood makes movies about things like me, and in those movies, the person is always a loner and/or a serial killer. Loner sounds pretty good. Serial killer, not so much. I'm not a fan of blood.

Besides cemeteries, hospitals are horrible places for me to visit. There's death all around. Death and spirits and things I don't exactly understand and don't want to understand. When it comes to death, nothing is easy. Not one thing. Not even the afterlife.

And the souls here, lots of them are sad. Like they are waiting for someone. Maybe a loved one who's gone on before, or a loved one who didn't make it in time to say goodbye. I don't know what the lady next to the fountain in front of the hospital is waiting for. Her hospital gown is blowing in the breeze, and her wrists are nearly slashed off. Surely she didn't do that to herself. Wait, would it be worse to hope she didn't do it to herself, or wish that someone did it to her?

I want my mommy.

"See anything?" Abel has been so quiet I almost forgot he was there, which shows how distracted I am by the amount of blood spilling into the fountain. Blood only I can see. I'm a lucky devil.

"No photographers as far as I can tell. We must have lost them, or they lost interest. Either way, I'm totally fine with that."

"I don't mean photographers."

I stop in my tracks and stare at him. He walks a few paces ahead of me before he turns around and places his hands in his pockets. "What?"

"Why would you ask me that?"

"Because it's a hospital, and people die in hospitals. Which means ghosts. Didn't you learn anything from your father on *Dark and Deadly Things*?"

I clear my throat and look him dead in the eye. I'm not having this conversation with him. "Doesn't mean I'd see them if they were here. People don't see ghosts."

He raises a brow at me.

"Okay, they do, but not all the time. I'm not some sort of a ghost magnet or anything." As far as I know. Who knows what I am besides a freak.

And because I'm a bitch and can't leave well enough alone, I just have to add more and twist the knife harder. "People who watched *Dark and Deadly Things* were idiots. Pure and simple. As were the people who called them and asked for help."

"What does that mean?" His expression instantly contorts from jovial to pained anger.

"It means that people are gullible enough to believe anything." I brush by his shoulder as I walk by, instantly feeling the electricity between us. Is that electricity or disdain for him at this moment? Who knows? All I know is I want to be anywhere but here. The best thing for me to do is keep Abel irritated at me, hate me even. He shouldn't be laughing or making jokes with me. I shouldn't be making him laugh so hard he cries. His family is dead, and he shouldn't be leaning on me to distract him from that fact. I'm in no way one who can offer sound ways to deal with the death of a parent. I'm not dealing with the loss of my mom well either.

But I know one thing for certain: Abel Hale can't be my friend. He can't. It would hurt too much.

And I know one more thing: the lady next to the fountain jumped.

CHAPTER SEVEN

CENTERVILLE MEMORIAL HOSPITAL ISN'T AS STATE of the art as hospitals in Nashville or Knoxville. Heck, Cookeville, a few towns over, has a better hospital than we do. But Centerville is ours, and it does the job.

The original building was a basic two-story structure with a clinic on the bottom and surgery and recovery rooms on top. As the town grew, so did the hospital. It's now six stories tall and has different wings devoted to different things. There's a maternity wing, an ICU wing, and even a burn unit.

And then there's the crazy wing.

I suppose that isn't nice of me to call it that.

It's the psychiatric wing. My father has been there since the incident.

I'm sure he'll be there for a lot longer. Centerville Memorial—as it was explained to me—doesn't keep lifelong mental patients, especially those who have been charged with serious crimes. Strangely, the murder of five people fits that criterion. Who knew? My sarcasm is going to get me in trouble some day.

Eventually, and I don't know how soon, my father will be

moved to Hartsville Prison for the Criminally Insane.

For some reason, the name reminds me of the asylum from Batman.

I shiver. I hope he doesn't become a criminal mastermind with the Riddler. Oh what capers they could plan...

What in the world did I ever do to deserve this life?

Abel is holding the giant glass door open for me. He's not looking at me though. Good. After what I said about all people who called my dad for help being morons, Abel shouldn't look at me. He shouldn't even be holding the door for me. I wouldn't hold the door for me.

He's tall enough to look over me, and his gaze is cast right on the fountain. I look too, even though I know what I'm going to see. The girl's hair is floating on top of the water. I don't see the rest of her.

"What's wrong?" I ask, fighting the urge to wave my fingers in front of his face to get his attention. I don't think I know him well enough to do that.

"Nothing." His eyes, those puppy dog green ones, look sad. Like there's something physically hurting him, and he can't stop it. I imagine it has to do with his family. It has to be about his family, right? Even though I was a bitch and said his parents were morons for calling my dad, I do miss his laugh and smile. Maybe I rushed into this he-needs-to-hate-me thing too soon? Especially going into this hospital, which for me will be like walking through the saddest, bloodiest, most horrific haunted house ever.

"Let's go." He motions me inside, and with a last somber gaze toward the fountain, he closes the door behind us.

CHAPTER EIGHT

NINETEEN NINETY-TWO CALLED AND WANTS its décor back.

Now, I understand the quality of a hospital doesn't depend on what the facility looks like. A place can be done up to the nines in finery and the latest whatever and still have horrible service and create an unpleasant experience.

However, this place with its pastel wallpaper, pointed wall protrusions in the strangest of places, and carpet Pee Wee Herman would be proud of, doesn't give off much of a you-can-trust-us-to-take-care-of-you vibe.

Abel heads through the *Saved by the Bell*-inspired carpet and toward the elevators like this isn't his first time here. It might not be for all I know. It isn't like we converse very much. I've only been here a handful of times, and on all those occasions, all the dead people made me want to run away screaming.

The lady next to the elevator smiles at me. Her teeth are black and rotting.

She's not a ghost… just a visitor like me.

Sometimes even the living can look worse than the dead. I'm sure I do at times, or most of the time, if I want to be honest with myself.

And who doesn't want to be honest with themselves?

Abel hits the up button, and he, our new black-toothed friend, and I all look at the elevator doors, waiting and willing them to open and put us out of our stranger-anxiety meeting.

Luckily, and I mean that in every sense of the word, the hospital has easy listening jazz playing through the speakers.

Ah. I feel nice and calm.

If only.

The elevator doors open, and a family of two small kids and a man and woman exit. The kids are bouncing up and down like they've had all the sugar in the world. The parents, their eyes are red like they've been crying. The old lady behind them—with her gown, her IV pole, and her glitching static ghost self—can't seem to keep up the pace.

The family heads out the door into the cloudy day, and the adults hold hands as the woman puts her head on the man's shoulder. It would be a sweet scene, if the old woman didn't fall to her knees and silently weep at the door. Some ghosts can't leave where they died. I don't know why. I don't make the rules. From what I can tell, there's like an invisible field around them, and there's no way to cross it. The old lady falls to her knees at the door. She's going to be stuck here for the rest of her afterlife.

"Come on, Elise." Abel places his hand on the small of my back and gently leads me through the doors. The tenderness of his touch sends electricity through my body, and I tilt my head up toward him. He doesn't return the gesture, and once we're inside the elevator, he moves his hand from my back.

The doors close.

The woman is weeping.

We're alone.

"Where's the old woman?"

"What old woman?" he asks as an afterthought. He

pushes the fifth floor button and steps back.

"The old woman who was standing next to us waiting for the elevator. The one with the black teeth."

He moves until his back is against the wall as the same easy-jazz music as was in the lobby filters through the elevator. "There was no old woman."

My heart skips a beat. Literally, it skips, and my breath catches in my throat. I've seen ghosts for years. Years! And never have I mistaken one for a real life person. I mean, how? How could I not know?

"Gotcha." A ghost—pun intended—of a smile pulls on his lips, and his eyes cut to me ever so slightly. He was kidding. He was kidding?

"Are you serious?"

"No."

"No, you aren't serious now, or you weren't serious then?"

He picks this time to keep quiet.

I shake my head and lean back against the wall. It's taking forever to get to level five.

"You're kidding." I sigh, with half a mind to smile back. I would smile. At one time, I might even flirt. I don't think this is the right time, though. His jacket is gone, more than likely left in his car. And his tie is gone. The first two buttons of his shirt are unbuttoned, and if I were the type of girl to notice such things, I'd notice how his pants fit him in all the right places, and how I wanted to look at his arm muscles forever. But I'm not the type of girl who flirts or thinks such things, so I don't.

Stop looking at his arms, I tell myself.

"You're being very calm about this." It's a true statement. I can't imagine the sadness and anger going through him right now, especially given what I said to him earlier. I know how much I had when my mom died, and I still had my father. Abel has no one. How does one even process that? How does someone move on from that? I guess if you're Abel Hale, you sweet talk the daughter of the man accused of killing your family into seeing the man accused of killing your family.

Yeah, this will totally end up well.

"I don't feel calm," he says in a calm voice. Irony and all. "I feel as far from calm as I can get."

"Could have fooled me." I sigh.

"I have," he says cryptically.

"What does…?" I can't finish my sentence because apparently my life is a soap opera, and I can't have a conversation with someone without being interrupted. Next time, we will talk about this—if there is a next time. Abel promised that after he talked to my father, he'd leave us alone and never bother us again. After today, I won't see him anymore. Thinking about that still breaks my heart.

I have no idea why. I shouldn't care. Maybe because I feel empathy for him, or maybe, I don't know, we have this connection I can't explain. There's something there, something not romantic. I don't know him well enough for that, but I'm not sure what the right word is. Familiar, I suppose. There's something familiar about him. He's the total opposite of Silas Ford, at least before Silas went crazy a few months ago.

Speaking of…

"Psyche ward," Abel reads aloud the sign welcoming us after the doors open.

When I saw my dad a few days ago, I promised myself I'd come back and visit him every day. Yes, I hated him, but I didn't think he killed those people. He needed someone on his side, and by golly, that someone was going to be me. That was a promise I broke almost immediately.

Abel walks in first. I follow. I figure if he's in front, he can do all the talking. Sounds good to me. I'll just stay in the back and watch the proceedings. We turn right at the elevator and end up at the nurses' station. The nurses' station is a big round circle of desks at the center of a large hallway.

Currently, it's being manned by one redheaded female nurse who looks to be in her mid-thirties. She's writing on a chart, sweat beading on her forehead. Another nurse, a blonde who's extremely beautiful in that over-trying way—in her case, it works—is sitting with her legs on the table and her feet in the air as she files down her fingernails.

The nurse who's actually working seems annoyed. I do believe I can relate. Some people in this world work for everything they have. They try so hard to be good and do the right thing, but it doesn't matter because the other person will always be picked first, the favorite of all who come in contact with her.

Abel raises a brow at me. Did he notice it too?

"Roger Morgan." I'm as bright and cheerful as I can be.

Just the mention of my father's name makes the nurse who's filing her nails stop mid-swipe. The nurse who's filling out the charts blinks a few times at me like she's trying to process what I said or didn't hear me right. Oh no, she heard me. Roger Morgan.

"He can't have visitors," the working nurse says, making me like her less than I had a few minutes ago.

"I know that…"

She isn't finished. "And especially not some kids who are here to get pictures of him when he's at his most vulnerable. You two should be ashamed of yourselves."

Working nurse, I see on her shirt that her name is Olivia, seems scarily attached to my father. She's young and full of ideas on how things should go here, I do believe. The other nurse, who's put her file back down, is my new favorite. I think she's been here long enough to know that some rules are made to be broken, that's just the way it is.

I can feel my ire rising. I've had a rough day, a rough week—hell, a rough life—and this little woman is going to tell me I should be ashamed of myself? That I should feel bad for wanting to talk to my father. I'll let her have it. I'll tell her and her colleague off. Not to do any good, but to make myself feel better.

I'm all ready to tell her this when a wave of calm washes over me. I don't know where it comes from, but I can't say I hate it. Well, I do hate it because it makes me forget all about the anger I had a few minutes ago. I'm calm. I'm happy. I'm...

Wait, what's happening to me?

"Ma'am." Abel flashes his kilowatt smile. Ole Olivia obviously approves. "This is Elise Morgan. I'm Abel Hale."

"Abel Hale!" The non-working nurse, her name tag reads Susan, sits up so quickly in her chair that she nearly knocks everything down around her. "I knew I recognized you! And you are..." She points directly at me. "You are his daughter."

I raise a brow very high.

"I mean not *his*, but Roger Morgan's. You're Elise. I've seen you on television a few times, back when *Dark and Deadly Things* was actually good."

Back when it was good; I have to smile at that. Some say, and I happen to believe them, that the show's heyday was about four years ago, before I found out about my dad faking evidence. I loved being a part of the show then, being with my dad, traveling, finding new and interesting locations to film.

Those were the good ole days. I just wish I'd realized it back then.

"Please, I don't want anyone to know we're here. I need to talk to my father. It's urgent."

Nurse Oliva tilts her head ever so slightly to the right and sighs. "Miss, I'm sorry, but your father hasn't been coherent since they brought him in. He's been in and out of episodes. Some days he thinks he's seeing ghosts, and the next he's trying to beat his head in the wall, saying he has bugs crawling around in there and has to get them out. The doctor said absolutely no visitors."

"I'm his daughter." That should trump everything.

"I'm sorry."

"I don't want your sorry. I want to see my father!" I'm way too loud, and my voice echoes through the quiet hallway. I can be louder if I have to be. These nurses have no idea how I can be if I'm pushed. *I* have no idea how I can be if I'm pushed.

Abel looks impressed. Good. That makes this all better—that's sarcasm, by the way. I don't think there's anything that can make this better.

Part of me wishes the nurses will put their foot down, call security, and have us escorted from the hospital. If that happens, we won't have to see my dad, Abel won't get to talk to him, and if I ride this out, it'll all be over soon—as much as it can be over. Another part of me, really wants to see my dad and make sure he's okay. I know he can't be totally okay being in here, but I need to know that he's all right. I might not like the man at the moment, but I do worry about him. Maybe if I see him, I can talk some sense into him? Maybe get him to snap out of it?

It's a small piece of hope that I hold onto. If I could get through to him, then everything would be okay, right? He could tell the police what really happened—that there was a black mass in the room with him.

And then he'd be right back in here. There's no upside.

"We have orders," Nurse Olivia says.

I'd like to show her some orders.

Abel places his hand on my shoulder, and I feel calm again. I like it when he touches me. It's like a peace washes over me. I haven't felt peace in so long that I'd love for Abel to keep his hand on me all the time. Not that that sounds creepy or anything.

"Ma'am, I understand you have orders, and you're very wise to follow them, but you see…" He gently rubs his fingers against her hand, and she lets him without slapping him. The way she swallows hard lets me know she enjoys it as much as I do when he touches me. Some people have a gift. "Elise and

I, we need to talk to her father. It's important to us, and it'll just be a few minutes."

"There's a guard down there," she says almost in a daze.

"Olivia!" The other nurse admonishes. Too bad Abel doesn't have another hand hidden in his body somewhere that he could use to make her feel calm too.

"Then you need to make the guard move so we can sneak in." Abel's voice is calming.

I bet he has no trouble getting the ladies. He can probably make them do whatever he wants during sex. *Yes, sir. Turn me over and smack my ass.*

Olivia takes a deep breath and licks her lips. I swear she's daydreaming about Abel and his magic fingers. "Go on down. I'll let you in his room. But you can only stay a few minutes, okay?"

"You can't be serious." Non-Olivia is suddenly very aware of the rules in this place. "You'll get us both fired."

Olivia turns toward her less than moral, from what I can tell, colleague. "Sister, we need to talk…"

CHAPTER NINE

FIVE MINUTES LATER, WE'RE STANDING AT the door to my father's room. The guard is being entertained by Not-Olivia, and Olivia is manning the desk. Olivia has Abel's cellphone number in case something comes up and we need to high tail it out of there. She's already unlocked my father's door.

"Blackmail is a wonderful thing." Abel winks at me.

"Apparently." Who knew Nurse Olivia knew everything the other nurse had ever done and had threatened to tell the big wigs if she didn't let us go see my father? Cause I overheard their not-so-quiet whisperings... and wow. I guess we all have secrets.

Olivia may be nice, but she's also practical. She could only give us five minutes at the most. So here we are, at the door, needing to go inside and talk to my father about things. My hand is on the knob... and I can't do it. I can't open it. I don't want to see him or talk to him.

I'm afraid, okay? I'm afraid, and I hate it.

"You can do this." Abel reassures me. His hand rests on the small of my back.

I think he's right. I think I can do this.

"Please don't ask him about my mother." I remind him of our deal.

"Your mother isn't who I'm curious about." Abel gently takes my hand off the door and opens it himself.

The door, as old and out-of-date as this entire hospital, creaks on its hinges as it protests being opened.

This is it. It's time to face the music and my father. I have to be brave. Brave? How stupid is that? Roger Morgan is my father. He'd never hurt me intentionally. I mean, yeah, he broke my heart and my trust, but that was then. He needs me now. I'm not going to let him down.

I've done that enough.

Truthfully, I need to know answers too, probably even more than Abel.

My father isn't tied down to the bed, which is a welcome sight. I relax some as I enter the room, and it isn't until the creaky door behind us closes that I realize this is probably a bad idea. I mean, my father isn't exactly stable.

He hunts ghosts for a living.

My dad is sitting in a chair. He isn't looking in our direction, but I can see his profile as he sits and stares out the bar-protected window. The sun has momentarily broken through the clouds. The last hurrah before the predicted rain takes over this afternoon. The warm glow of the sunshine envelops him, and he looks like a plant soaking it all in. It seems peaceful. Hopefully, this will be a quiet visit, a nice visit.

He's wearing blue scrubs, not the white ones like he had on before. His beard is growing out. It looks funny to see him without his signature goatee. He still doesn't have any hair on his head.

Abel nudges me to go farther inside.

I reluctantly comply.

My heart's beating a thousand miles a minute. I don't know what to say or do. I should have thought about this before I walked in, truth be told. I got Abel in here. Now what's going to happen?

"Talk to him," Abel whispers in my ear.

Easier said than done. My mind won't form coherent words. What are you supposed to say in situations like these? "Dad?" It's the best I can come up with.

He flinches ever so slightly, so I keep going, "Dad, it's me, Elise. Do you know who I am?"

He doesn't answer.

My heart sinks.

Abel pulls out a chair for me, and I sit down so close to my dad I could reach out and touch him if I wanted. I'm too scared to try. "Dad, it's Elise. Your daughter. Can you hear me?"

Nothing.

I knew this was a waste of time. We never should've come here. I stand up to tell all of this to Abel and leave.

Abel has other ideas. "Roger, I'm Abel Hale. You were at my house, do you remember that?"

Another flinch.

Abel needs to be very careful what he says. My father might appear to be a gentle giant, but looks can be very deceiving. "I need to ask you a few questions about what happened at my house," Abel says as he squats next to my father. Abel doesn't seem as scared of my father as I am. Abel places his hand on my father's shaking knee.

Another flinch, and Dad's nose flares. He remembers that night. Sure he does. I bet he can't forget it. I bet it runs through his scrambled mind constantly. I don't know if this is the best thing to be talking about right now, though. We have to talk about it, but it would've been nice to lead into it.

I raise my finger to Abel to tell him to chill out. He doesn't take the hint.

"Roger, I need to know what you saw. I mean, I was there. I… I can't explain it. I need answers, and you're the only person in the world who can give them to me."

My father's jaw clenches.

"Roger, please." I can tell Abel grips Dad's leg tighter. "What was in that house with us? What did you pick up on the EVPs? Was it evil? I felt it. You said it wouldn't hurt us... you said!"

I stand up and put my hands on Abel's shoulder. "Calm down." I order, but it seems I don't have the same effect on him as he does on me.

"I need answers, Elise." He almost growls.

"I do too, trust me. But I don't think we'll find them here."

"What happened? Did you know?" He stands up and looms over my father. "Did you know what was in my house? Was it all for show!"

Abel doesn't back down. I slide until I'm in front of him. I have to hold him back from going after my father. My hands are on Abel's chest, and I'm pushing as hard as I can. I don't think it's doing any good. I know if Abel wanted, he could have me out of his way in no time with little effort.

"Move out of the way." He sneers. His tone is dangerous.

"No." I don't feel brave, but I sure hope I look it. I won't let him hurt my father. He's all I have left.

"Elise..." Abel closes his eyes, and his jaw clenches. He can be mad all he wants, but I won't let him go after my father. Abel runs his fingers through his hair and marches back toward the door. My chest hurts, my stomach hurts... every muscle in my body is at the ready. I should have trusted my gut. This is exactly how I expected this to go down. Of course there would be a fight. Why did I think anything else?

Stupid feelings.

Abel has his back to me, taking big deep breaths. I think he's trying to calm himself. Lord, I hope he is. I don't want to have to fight him again. The nurse won't be able to keep the guard occupied for long. We need to get out of here and fast.

Still, I have some questions for my father too. There are so many things I'm not sure about, so many things that need to make sense and don't.

The first thing I need to know is what. What in the world happened that night?

I turn to face my father when my nose runs into his chest. I scream and cover my mouth so no one outside will hear me.

My father is standing straight and tall, looking down at me with that disapproving scowl he used to have when I was little. *Elise, I told you to remember your backpack! I don't have time to go home and get it! Don't tell people you can see ghosts! They'll think you're crazy.*

Self-fulfilling prophecy, that one.

He's towering over me. I'm nearly flush with him, and all I want to be is away. I back up, and he follows. I've never been afraid of my father. Never, but this… this thing right at this moment isn't my father. He's something I don't recognize. Something I need away from now. A stranger.

I keep stepping.

He keeps stepping.

I'll run out of the room soon.

"Dad?" My hand is still covering my mouth, so my voice is a muffled quiver. "Dad, what's going on? What do you remember?"

This is stupid. My father would never hurt me, just like he never hurt those people in that house. I'm acting irrationally, and I'm not going to do it anymore.

I dig my heels into the ground and refuse to move. Not at all. If he wants to hurt me, then fine. But I'm not running from him. I came here for answers, and damn it, I'm getting them.

Just as I decide to be a badass, Abel steps in front of me and blocks me from my father. This isn't the time for Abel to be all big and chauvinistic. It's time for him to back the hell up. I'm sorry I went all wimp for a few seconds. I hadn't known Dad was behind me. But I know now. I'm calm now, and I'll be fine. Abel needs to back up.

"Abel, I have this."

"What happened in the house, Roger?" I hear the frustration, the anger, the grief in the way his voice cracks.

How much can my father even say? Can he even talk?

Just then, the scariest feeling—the scariest thought—in the world washes over me. What if... what *if* my father *is* the man who killed all those people? What if he did something? I don't know what, but what if he's responsible?

What if he snapped after my mom died?

What if this is all on him, and we're in here taunting him?

I mean, really, what's more plausible? The fact that my father lost his mind and started hacking everyone to death or that a ghost did it? Or a poltergeist? If I were a betting woman, I'd say all roads lead to my father being guilty. And the way he's acting now is downright terrifying.

No, he couldn't have. He couldn't...

My dad is a lot of things—liar, thief, cheat—but he's not a killer. I know he's not.

I peek around Abel's arm and stare into my father's blank, dead eyes.

He's not a killer.

I want to believe it.

He's making it very difficult.

Then an even more terrifying thought consumes me: what if my father had been possessed?

What if he still is?

"The horseless man... the horseless man... the horseless man..." My dad starts repeating over and over. Each time has a different inflection, a different tune, a different voice.

"What's the horseless man?" I whisper to Abel, who shakes his head.

"What are you talking about, Roger? We don't understand you."

My father's head stops shaking. He stands slightly

straighter and looks Abel dead in the eye. "You trusted the wrong man."

Silence.

Abel shrugs at me but looks like he wants to throw up.

"You trusted the wrong man!" my father yells, making Abel and me both jump.

I hate this room. I hate this place. I hate being in here with him. I want out. Now. I can feel the anxiety welling up inside me. Higher and higher… more and more until I want to scream. I want out. I back toward the door, ready to bolt. I can't do this. "He's come home. He's come home." My father sings. He starts humming music only he can hear, puts his arms up like he's dancing with someone, and begins waltzing around the little corner of his room. "He's come home. He's come home." Over and over, he sings.

I don't see anyone he's dancing with—I mean, no ghosts. There is no one, nothing. My dad truly has lost his mind.

"Roger. Come on. This is a good act. But I need you to know that I don't believe you. I know you're making all this up to cover up what you did, what really happened? Aren't you?"

"You trusted the wrong man." He twirls. "She's come home."

She?

"Roger!" Abel stomps toward my dad and grabs him by the wrists.

I run over to stop Abel. He's strong, I'll give him that, but I'm determined. I grab his wrists and wrestle him away from my father. I don't have to try very hard. Seconds later, Abel lets my dad go. Abel's face turns a sickening pale, and he's out the door in two seconds flat, leaving me in there with *Dancing with the Stars*.

"Dad?" I pray for him to answer me. Not the act he put on in front of Abel—please, it had to be an act—but for my dad to answer me the way I know he can. The way where he's not pretending. He can't be pretending, please don't let him be pretending.

I want my father back.

My real father.

I want my mom.

I want this all to be over with.

Is that too much to ask?

Apparently, it is.

My dad stops dancing, stops humming. He takes a step closer to me, bends down until his hands are on his knees. I lean closer to hear what he has to say. There has to be something. Something he wants to tell me that he couldn't in front of Abel.

My father gets as close to me as he can. He raises his hand and bops my nose.

His high-pitched, maniacal laughter echoes through his tiny room. That's it. I'm done with this. His icy-cold hand grabs my wrist before I can leave, and he pulls me toward his chest. His hand covers my mouth so I can't scream. Abel is long gone by now. My dad pulls me as close to him as he can, his lips centimeters from my ear.

"She's coming for you," he whispers. "Coming for him. She didn't think it through. A price for two."

Why does that sound familiar? "Who?" I whisper back, shaking.

My dad giggles. "All choices have consequences, children. Consequences... good intentions... the road to hell. She's coming for you. Carol knows the way."

My breath catches. "Carol? Mom? What does Mom have to do with this? Dad, what is going on?"

He pushes me back hard against the wall, knocking the breath out of me. "Four not one... four," my dad says.

My back hurts, but I fight to suck in a breath. "Dad, what are you saying? What did you do?"

"Not me. Her." He shakes his head and digs his nails into

his scalp so deep blood starts to trickle out. "A price for two."

My phone starts singing, and I pull it out of my pocket. Silas Ford is texting me. What the hell does he want? I start to open the message.

Dad stops me. "Don't trust Silas. Don't trust Silas. Don't trust Silas."

"What? Why? Why can't I trust Silas! Dad, what did he do to you?"

"The horseless man isn't real. Not now." Dad points at me, and blood drips down the tips of his fingernails and drops to the floor. "They are coming after you."

"Who is?" I practically scream! Enough going around and around in these endless circles.

"She tried so hard."

I shake my father's shoulders. "Who tried? Who is coming after me?"

Dad blinks a few times as his eyes glaze over white. "She made a mistake."

CHAPTER TEN

I RUN OUT THE DOOR AND don't stop when I reach Abel. He yells my name even when I pass Olivia and Not-Olivia. The elevators will take too long. I run.

My phone is firmly clutched in my hand as I burst through the door to the stairs and race down to the first floor.

I make it to floor two before I collapse in the stairwell and start to cry.

I thought I'd been so brave up until now. I'd held it in. I hadn't cried. Not even at my mom's funeral. I've kept busy at school, focused on my work and getting good grades. I took care of my grandma's house for my mom. I knew she'd like it if I did. She had all her grandmother's antiques in there. I dust them at least twice a week. I keep everything neat and tidy because that's what my mom would have wanted.

I've been more organized than I've ever been in my life.

I have planner after planner after planner of things written down so I don't forget. I can't forget.

I can't forget her or that night. I can't forget the cold I felt, the presence, the mass being thrown against the wall.

The police.

The hospital.

The questions.

I start shivering. I'm so cold I don't think I'll ever warm up. It isn't cold in this stairwell. It is me. *The horseless man. She's coming for you. She made a mistake.*

I pull my knees up to my chest and rock as silent tears fall down my cheeks. I don't know what my dad was talking about or if I should even believe him. I don't know what to believe anymore. When someone sees ghosts as much as I do, they just sort of lose the ability to tell real from fantasy, the natural from the supernatural. Everything is a blur.

Nothing is right.

I can't stop shaking.

And I can't stop crying.

My hair is sticking to my face, and I don't care. I don't care about anything because there's nothing to care about anymore. Dad is gone. Mama is gone. It's just me alone in this world, and I have no idea what to do or how to even go on. I can't get out of this damn hospital right now. I may just sit in this stairwell and die here. Then I'll become one of the hospital ghosts and wander aimlessly forever.

I might as well.

I'm wandering aimlessly right now.

Pressure on my shoulder scares the hell out of me. I jump like I've been shot and move away from whatever is holding me down. In my experience with the paranormal, it can be anything holding me down. I know one thing for sure: I'll fight the bastard off as hard as I can. I might wallow myself to death in this stairwell, but I'll be damned if I'm killed in here. If anyone is going to kill me, it's going to be me.

Girl power and all.

"Elise, it's me. Stop. You're going to hurt yourself." Abel lets me go and backs away with his hands held high in the air. Probably a good move on his part.

Why did he have to find me? Why couldn't he have let

me wallow here in my own cocoon of guilt and anguish until the last bits of breath left my body?

I sound entirely too overly dramatic.

"What are you doing here?" I wipe my eyes with the back of my hand. Thankfully, I hadn't started to ugly cry yet. My nose isn't running that I know of. That would be embarrassing. I guess I do care a little.

"You ran by me like a bat out of hell. What happened in there anyway?"

"You should've stuck around and found out." I wipe my eyes and pray that I can even stand. It's no fun wallowing in a stairwell with two people. Wallowing is a solitary sport, which I will continue when I get back to my dorm. I just hope Naked Girl will let me wallow in peace.

I've earned it after today.

"Yeah, sorry about that. I just couldn't take it anymore. I didn't trust myself."

That was unexpected. "You couldn't trust yourself? Why?"

He clears his throat. Seems Mr. Abel Hale is hiding something. "Nothing. Not really. I was just getting too mad, and as much as I want answers from your dad, it doesn't mean that you should have to see me yell at him or do something we'd both regret."

I shrug. "I yelled at him *and* did something I regret."

I regret telling my dad I didn't want to be his daughter anymore right after Mom died. That was a low blow he didn't deserve. Yes, he faked evidence in all those cases. Yes, he put my mom and me in danger at the house mom died in, but that didn't mean he was any less my dad. I'll regret all of that until my dying day. Which, since Abel has come and bothered my wallowing, won't be today.

Thanks dude.

"Well..." I stand and straighten my dress. It has gotten more wear today than I thought. "I guess you can go now."

"Go? Where am I going?"

"You are leaving, remember? You said after you talked to my father that you'd leave me alone and never bother me again." I don't want him to leave me alone, and I sure don't want him to never bother me again. Maybe I'm reaching or projecting or something, but he's all I have. This one guy I don't even know is my only link to humanity because, let's face it, my only other friend is a naked ghost I can't even talk to.

And Silas.

I guess he's my friend.

Or not if I'm supposed to believe my dad.

I'd forgotten all about Silas's text message. Ignoring all proper etiquette rules, I check my message right in front of Abel. Good thing no one has manners anymore.

So sorry about your dad. Listen, the network wants to talk to us about continuing the show. After a few months, so we can give everyone a chance to grieve, of course. They want you on camera. You in? There are so many people already on the waiting list to get their houses investigated. They're scared. Can't blame them. We need to talk.

I read the message five times before Abel interrupts me. "Who is it?"

"Silas." I see no need to hide it.

"I thought y'all had broken up."

"We have." My mind is swimming, and I feel like I'm in a daze. Ghost hunting is like the mob… you can get out, but they try to get you right back in.

"Anything important?" Abel is staring at me like he can't get a read on me.

I have news for him. I can't get a read on me either.

"No. Nothing." I turn my screen off and put my phone back in my bag. "So, I guess this is goodbye."

He bites his lip, and his eyes narrow. I swear he's trying to read me. I'm an open book. Course, even I don't know what all the chapters are about. "Can we get out of the stairwell first before we say our goodbyes? This seems a little, I don't know, depressing."

"I can't remember a time that wasn't." I sigh. It's been a very long time since anything seemed happy. Slowly, everything has descended into a gray and black world that hurts my head and my heart.

We'll walk out, Abel and me. We'll say pleasant goodbyes at his car. Then we'll go our separate ways. Easy. Simple.

And it should be easy and simple because I don't know Abel that well. And by *that well*, I mean not at all. It should be incredibly easy.

It is anything but.

Abel's lip quirks sheepishly at me, and he places his hand on my back to lead me down the stairs. Guess I won't be dying in the stairwell after all.

Hooray?

We get down the last two flights of stairs and open the door leading to the lobby. It's the same lobby where we came in. Same floors, same easy-jazz music. I could so go to sleep listening to this. Maybe I should play it at home when I can't sleep and have tried everything else.

The old woman is still on her knees. She's clutching her IV pole and silently screaming at her family, who have been gone at least an hour. This will be her life now. This and nothing else.

She looks at me as we go by.

Her eye is full of pain. The static rolls across her body. This is it for her. Her very own personal hell.

She screams at me to help.

Abel turns me away from her and holds me tight to his chest. We don't stop walking.

CHAPTER ELEVEN

ABEL HUGS ME TIGHTLY AND RUBS his hand over my forehead. He picks up the pace, and we're past the fountain and walking through the parking lot in record time. It's so fast that I don't get a chance to see the ghost in the fountain. I'm not sad about that. Once we get close to his car, he lets me go. I'm no longer holding on to him, no longer touching him.

I feel exposed somehow. Like everything would be all right, and then bam, I'm hit with the real world again.

"You all right?" He bends down to look me in the eye. He puts his hands on each side of my face. His hand provides much needed warmth to my skin.

"Elise, answer me. Are you okay?"

"Yeah, I'm fine." I'm not fine. In fact, I feel a little woozy. I can't remember the last time I felt like this. Then again, it's been a long time since I've seen this many spirits or had this much excitement in one day.

I think this proves that I lead a very boring life. "Did you see her?"

"Who?"

"The ghost in the lobby? Did you see her?" No sense in

denying it now. "You saw her, didn't you? How else would you have known to run me out of there?"

"You were freaking out about your father."

"I was not…"

"And I figured it would be gentlemanly to get you out."

"And past the fountain ghost and to the parking lot where there aren't any ghosts at the moment." I squint my eyes at him, willing my fingers and toes to stop shaking. It isn't Abel that's causing my issues. It's me. Something is happening inside of me. "And you expect me to believe you don't see them too."

Abel's gaze is steely hard, and I wish I'd never brought it up. Course cat's out of the bag now. So much for keeping that secret. Me and my big stupid mouth. To be fair, to me, he did seem to imply that I saw ghosts when he ran me past them, and I went with it. I assumed. Stupid assuming. He probably thinks I'm as crazy as my father now.

Since I've blabbed my one big secret about myself, I might as well ask the hard question. "Abel, answer me. Do you see them too?"

"No," he says abruptly before opening the car door for me. "Get in."

He doesn't look me in the eye. I'm not sure I believe him.

"Get in? Why?"

"I'm taking you back to your dorm, unless you have somewhere else you'd like to go."

That's incredibly sweet of him, considering I'm about to have a nervous breakdown any minute. I don't know if I can go back to my dorm with him. Or even if I should. I can feel the photographers around. They're hiding, I bet. Ready to shoot the tender moment between the victim and the villain's daughter. We'll be on the lead news tonight for sure. I'm trying to find it in me to care.

"I can get a cab."

"I know you can. But I have a car, and I would… look, I'd

like to spend time talking to you that doesn't involve some kind of horror. Do you think we can do that?"

Nothing would make me happier. "If you think we can." It's my incredibly cool answer.

"Then get in." He motions for me to do just that, and I comply. It isn't every day a guy opens the car door for me. In fact, I don't think it's ever happened to me. I know Silas never did. Course, that's not saying a whole lot. Silas never did a whole lot of anything sweet after my mom died, and it's hard to remember what he was like before then.

I've got to stop comparing Abel to Silas. Silas is in the past. Abel will never be the future. I have to accept it and move on. The faster I do that, the better it will be for all of us.

I get in, willing my heart not to swoon as he closes the door behind me, and buckle my seatbelt. I've seen way too many ghosts who have died from car accidents to ever go anywhere without putting mine on.

The sun is still incredibly bright today, much too bright for November. I thought it was supposed to rain. Where are the clouds? I'm so ready for fall weather. This is getting ridiculous. Abel opens the door to get it. I pull the sun visor down to block the sun. When I do, I scream.

I wish they'd stop doing that.

From the reflection in the mirror of the sun visor, I see a ghost in the backseat, glitching to her heart's content. Only it isn't any ghost. It's my mom.

I haven't seen her since Halloween night, and here she is in the backseat of this car at this very moment.

This is my life. And my life sucks.

"What? What's wrong?" Abel grabs my hand and that awesome wave of calm hits me again. He needs to do this all the time. I could get addicted to it.

"It's nothing."

My mom glares.

I don't think she likes being called a nothing. I wouldn't

either.

"People don't scream at nothing. What do you see? Is there something in the car with us?"

I want so badly to say no. No, there is nothing in the car with us… nothing at all… nothing.

"It's my mom." I blurt out and instantly regret it.

"Your mom. Like the ghost of your mom, your mom."

I nod reluctantly. Why did I have to tell him? I mean, from what I can tell, he can sort of feel when something paranormal is around. If him running me through the hospital is any indication. But dang if I know what he knows. It isn't like he tells me nearly as much as I tell him, and I don't feel like I know him well enough to ask. Someday, I'll ask…

Someday.

"You know for sure she's dead?"

Hearing those words makes my heart hurt. I don't want to think about it, but yes, I do. "Oh yeah. I'm sure."

"But they never found her body." I can see the wheels turning in that brain of his.

"My mother and your mother are different." Course, they really aren't, but I'm not ready to tell Abel that yet. His mother is dead, just like mine is. I'm not going to be the one to tell him though. I can't deal with that kind of pressure right now.

He places both his hands firmly on the steering wheel and dances his fingers a few times. "Does that mean my mom is dead, too?" His voice cracks and it breaks my heart. Absolutely breaks it in half.

"I don't know." Our relationship is built on lies, is it not?

"You don't know, or you don't want to tell me?"

Oh that Abel Hale. He's the perceptive one. "Abel, the honest answer is that I have no idea what's going on. I don't know what happened in your house or that house where my mom went missing. I don't know what happened to my dad. Hell, I don't know what's happening to me. So, no, I have no idea what happened to your mom." That's as honest as I can be. I know she's dead. I don't know the cause.

"But you'd tell me if you did, right? You'd tell me if she was dead." He's testing me, working me over and trying to size me up.

I want him around, don't I? I don't want to be alone, and if he found out, he wouldn't need me. God, I sound so needy and pathetic.

My mom glitches behind me.

Would it be better to know what happened to her? Am I glad I see her, or would it be better not to know? I didn't have a choice, but Abel does. I can make it for him. I can save him days of pain before his world falls apart again.

Before I answer, I notice my mom is trying to speak. I turn around and try my hardest to read her lips. I don't think I'm very good at it. I need to see if she can do charades like Naked Girl does. I think Mom's mouthing, "Tell him."

I think she needs to mind her own business.

Abel nods a few times. I think he's fighting back tears. I didn't answer him. Why would he be crying?

"Okay, well what does your mom want?"

"I'm not sure. She shows up at random times."

"Are the times really random, or do you just not see the pattern?"

Good question. "I'm not sure."

"You aren't sure about a lot of things, are you?"

He doesn't wait for my answer before he speeds off toward the dorms.

I expected some sort of conversation, at the very least an interrogation. He just found out I see ghosts for goodness sakes. You'd think he'd have questions, concerns, doubts. Maybe he's playing along and doesn't believe me. Maybe he's testing me. Maybe he's using me to get access and information to my father.

My mind is racing, thinking about all negative and scary things. Abel drives in silence, past the businesses and houses that lead to Southern Tennessee University. The only time he glances in my direction is when we drive by the cemetery. His mom is still there. What is she waiting for?

Two seconds after we drive by, I see what his mom was waiting for. *My* mom disappears from Abel's backseat and glitches next to his mother at the cemetery gate. They turn toward me, both of them in eerie synchronicity.

They hold hands.

What in the...?

I unbuckle my seatbelt to get a better view through the rearview window. They know each other? Or is this some ghost solidarity thing.

"Elise! Hold on!"

I hear the words.

I feel the impact.

I sink into the nothingness.

CHAPTER TWELVE

"HEY, CAN YOU HEAR ME? ELISE? Can you hear me?"

Abel is tapping on my cheek, well, this close to smacking, but since I don't want to think of him as an abusive boyfriend, I'll go with tapping. He's saying my name all frantic when all I feel is calm.

Calm with a hint of head trauma.

"What happened?" I try to sit up. Immediately the world starts spinning, and I literally see stars. I decide that's a very bad idea.

"Hold on. Don't get up. I need to call 9-1-1."

"Ugh, why?" It isn't like I'm dying. My head feels a little off kilter, and it hurts like a mother, but I'll be all right. Did you wreck your car?"

"No, I swerved to miss a stray dog and you fell backwards. Hit your head pretty hard against the side window too. Why were you out of your seatbelt?"

"I don't remember."

I totally remember.

"Well, hold on. I'm calling for help."

"Wait, wait…" I put my hand on his, willing him to feel

the same calming sensation as I feel when he touches me. I don't think he does. "I'm fine. I really am. Nothing a good Tylenol and a few hours rest won't fix. I'll be fine. Is your car damaged?"

He sighs. I think he knows where I'm going with this. "No, but…"

"No buts. I promise I'm not hurt enough to go the hospital. I'll be fine."

"You live alone. What if you need something? What if something happens to you?"

"Awww. I didn't know you cared." It seems being hit in the head makes me an incredible flirty buffoon, who knew?

"I care enough not to want to see you die."

That doesn't seem like he cares very much. It makes me sad. Sadness makes my head hurt worse. "Still, I don't want to go to the ER."

"How about a doctor?"

"No."

"You hit your head pretty hard."

"I'll live."

"You sure?"

"Positive. Sixty to forty that I make it to tomorrow."

He actually laughs. His laugh, though pleasant and welcome, sends shockwaves through my head. Ouch. Ouchy ouch.

"I don't think those are good odds."

"They'll do. Look, we've been lucky today with the photographers and all that. We have. But we go to the ER, and things won't go so well. I don't want to go to Centerville Memorial either. I can't be in the same place as my dad. Not now." I try to turn around in my seat and get my bearings. I feel sticky. I look at my hand and see the blood. I'm going to be sick. "Please, just take me home."

"I don't think I should. You live all alone."

"Not true. I have Naked Girl."

Oh good Lord. Yes, I'm a walking—or in my case, sitting because I'm not sure I can walk—stereotype for someone with a head injury. Loose lips sink ships and all that jazz. Why don't I just tell him my entire life story while I'm at it?

"Naked Girl?"

"Never mind. Just drive. Please."

He doesn't seem to want to leave it alone. Why would I expect anything less? It ain't like we're just talking about the weather. "Is Naked Girl of the human variety?"

"At one time."

"Uh huh, and you expect her to take care of you?"

I'm getting sleepy, but I refuse to let Abel know it. I probably should go to the ER, but I don't want to. Naked Girl seems like the best option. I'm okay with that. Abel needs to get on board.

The blood on my hands blurs in my vision. "I think she'll do the best she can."

"Right." Abel sighs and starts the car back up. "I'm going to regret this," he says as he drives away, hopefully toward my house.

"Not in the least." I smile from ear to ear. I finally won a battle in my life. Hooray!

Ouch.

"So, tell me about Naked Girl."

I'd love to settle against my seat, but it hurts the back of my head too much. Then again, lying back might win out. Everything seems so light. So nice, so... calm. "She's a girl, and she's naked." That about sums her up.

"And she's a ghost?"

I don't answer that. I'm too busy in this happy haze I'm in.

"And you see her?"

"I'm not the only person who has ever seen a ghost." I remind him, though I'm the only person I know that sees them regularly. Most people *might* have one ghost sighting in their lifetime. Me? I have at least one a day.

"True." He has a mysterious air to his voice. I think he has a lot more questions.

Too bad I'm too tired to care.

I shut my eyes for a little rest.

That's it.

I'm not going to sleep.

I've got too much on my mind.

I'm not.

I'm…

CHAPTER THIRTEEN

IT'S SOFT.

I think it's soft.

And by it, I mean the thing I'm lying on.

And by soft, I mean relatively speaking because this isn't exactly the softest thing I've ever lain on.

It isn't my bed in my dorm. I know that much for certain. That thing is as hard as a rock.

And it isn't my bed at my grandmother's house. That bed has a down comforter that someone can sink into so deep they may never find their way out.

This is something different. Something I can't exactly place, and my eyes won't cooperate enough to stay open.

The back of my head hurts... the side of my head hurts.

Man, does it ever hurt.

Why does it hurt?

Why is there beeping?

Why is something pinching my arm on the inside of my elbow?

Wait...

He didn't... screw him, he didn't!

I roll my eyes around until I can focus on something, anything. The room I'm in has dull lighting, and it isn't exactly easy to find something to look at. Everything is gray or off-white, or I don't know, blah. This is the blahest room I've ever not seen.

I try to sit up, and big hands plop on my shoulders to hold me down. "Calm down. Be still. You'll pull out your IV." The big hands belong to Abel. The calmness falls over me like it had earlier. I fight it. I don't want to be calm. I don't think I should be calm at the moment. The opposite of calm seems the right thing to be right now.

Take that Abel Hale!

"You took me to the hospital." I still can't see. Shapes have no forms, nothing looks right, and the more I try to focus, the more distorted everything is.

"I took you to the hospital." Well, at least he admits it.

I'm going to smack him upside the head. I lean back against the pillow and squeeze my eyes shut. There's nothing I want more than to be in my dorm, in my room, with my earphones on and the world shut out.

He took me to the damn hospital.

There are no words for the frustration building inside me. The frustration has been building for the last six months, and I have a feeling it's going to unleash itself on Abel. I'm not going to stop it either. He took me to the freakin' hospital.

"I told you to take me home." I sound tired. I am tired.

"And that's exactly where I was taking you until you passed out."

"I fell asleep." Moron. Doesn't know the difference between sleeping and fainting.

"Uh-huh. Do you normally fall asleep so deeply that you can't be woken up?"

I cross my arms all defensive and stuff. "Yes."

"Even when someone shakes you, calls your name, pinches your butt?"

Wait… "You pinched my butt?"

"If you hadn't passed out, you'd know."

I can hear the smile in his voice. Jerk.

"That's illegal, to touch someone who is unconscious without their consent… I mean… you know what I mean."

"I know what you mean." I hear metal chair legs scraping against the floor. The sound makes my head feel like it's going to explode or, at the very least, bust my eardrums into tiny little pieces. Finally, when he's so close to the bed he could hold my hand if he wants, and he doesn't seem to want because I ain't felt it yet, he stops moving toward me.

"No, Elise, I didn't pinch any part of your body. But, I will admit that when I looked over and saw your head lolled to the side and you not responsive, I might have broken every land speed record to get you here."

"You did?" There's no way he'd care that much about me. Must be an obligation type thing. Didn't want a dead girl in his car, where I could haunt him forever. Seems I missed out on a golden opportunity. Darn it. I could've haunted the car of Abel Hale for the rest of his days or until he sold the car to a junkyard, and then I'd wander there aimlessly forever. Man, that sounds depressing.

"Course I did. Believe it or not, I do have a heart. I don't want anything bad to happen to you."

"In your car." I add because I'm snarky.

"In general." He sighs and leans back in the chair.

The beep… beep… beep… echoing through the room is starting to slow down. Guess my heart has decided I'm in a hospital and not some imaginable house of horrors.

Though they are the same thing in my opinion.

I try again to focus. The light above my bed illuminated the room some, but not enough to see very well. My eyes aren't helping with that endeavor either. "Please tell me I'm not at Centerville Memorial."

The thought of being in the same hospital as my dad

freaks me out, and my heart monitor goes into all kinds of fits. He puts his hand gently on my arm. "Shhh… it's okay."

Instant calm.

I wonder if there's a reason for that. Like we have some sort of connection. I don't have the time or the energy, or quite frankly the mental capacity, to figure that one out. All I know is if I'm at Centerville, it won't be okay, and nothing Abel says will make me think it is.

My mind is fighting with my heart, and I'm the one losing.

"You're in Mercy Medical. Chill. Not Centerville. I wouldn't do that to you."

Good to know he does have some compassion for me. "Good. Thank you."

He moves his hand from my arm. My heart monitors stay at a steady pace. I don't like having these things hooked up to me while I'm in the room with him. It's like a lie detector test—or an emotion barometer. I've never been one to wear my heart on my sleeves, and I don't want to start now. There's a reason I don't like to get too close to people. And, you know, the folks who complained to the network that I could be cold and distant at times probably had a good point.

"You don't have to thank me. Just don't ever scare me like that again."

"I make no promises." I mean it as a joke. I don't know if he takes it that way.

"Why were you turned around in my car, anyway? Did you see something besides your mother?"

I sigh and move my arm from covering my eyes. The world won't ever come into focus if I keep my eyes covered. I should sell that saying to Hallmark. Have them make me a card.

I refuse to tell him about his mother. It's probably wrong of me, and I'm sure I'll pay for it, but I don't want to do that to him. Not today. I will someday. But for now, I'd rather not.

There's already too much going on to tell him about his mother. God, I hope I'm making the right decision.

Maybe it's selfish.

Okay, it's very selfish. Still, I have my mind made up.

"I saw my mother. Standing outside the cemetery gates."

Not a total lie.

I'm making progress.

"What was your mother doing outside the cemetery gates? They never found her body, right?"

I don't answer right away. What do I say to that?

"I'm sorry. That was rude of me to say. I don't know how I'd feel if someone mentioned my mother, and here I am doing the same thing to you. I'm sorry."

He shouldn't apologize to me. Not after everything. Especially not after what I know. "Don't be sorry. It's just hard to talk about her, you know? No, they never found her body, but I can still see her. I know she's dead, but I can't tell anyone because they will... they do... think I'm crazy."

I can finally make out a television on the wall. A black, flat screen, not very big television. Despite all of that, it's the prettiest television I've ever seen. Hooray for progress.

"That has to be hard. No one believing you. Seeing things no one else sees, and not being able to tell anyone about it."

He's laying it on mighty thick. I wonder why. Is this some new tactic to get me to spill my beans on all things ghostly, or is he talking about something I have no idea about? It's probably the latter, and my mind is so jumbled I just don't see it.

Oh, look at that, a white board attached to the wall with words written in purple marker on it. I have no idea what the words are. That's not the point.

Words!

Time to change the subject. I'm not really in the mood to talk about our dead mothers. Seems legit. "Has a doctor been in here to see me?"

He sits up and rests his elbows on his knees. "Yeah, a few hours ago. Said you had a concussion, and they wanted to monitor you."

"A few hours?" Because that was the important part of that sentence. "How long have I been out?"

"Well, a long time. About six hours."

I sit up so fast all the progress I'd made with seeing totally disappears. The room starts spinning, and I swear little baby chickens are dancing the cancan around my head.

Ouch.

Just.

Ouch.

"Would you stop doing that? You're going to hurt yourself."

"I think I've already hurt myself, wouldn't you say?"

"I would say. And you don't want to do it anymore if you ever want to get out of here."

"I'd like to get out now. Think that can be arranged?"

He shakes his head and scoffs. Yeah. I feel the same way. "They wanted to keep you a few more hours for observation. They did some X-rays. I'm not sure what else."

I groan, lay my head back against the pillows that could totally use some more fluffing, and put my hand over my eyes that totally hate me right now. "I dread getting the bill."

"I'll pay it."

I peek out between my fingers and stare at him.

"What?" He shrugs.

"You're going to pay my hospital bill? Do you have any idea how much it'll be?"

"Do you have any idea how rich my family is?"

Well no, no I don't. I never thought about him being rich. I mean, I just never thought much about it. Hale House was a modest size house from what I could tell on television. A normal house, or at least I thought it was. So yeah, I know I'm not rich. I guess I never assumed he would be.

Doesn't matter if he is. No, I didn't want to come to the hospital, but he did the right thing bringing me here. I have to admit that begrudgingly. As bad as I feel right now, I'm glad he brought me here instead of home. I don't think Naked Girl could've helped me. I doubt it anyway, although she might have some skills I don't know about.

"I can't take your money."

"It's mine to give. I don't have anyone else to spend it on." I can hear the pain in his voice. I feel it too. I don't have anyone else either. We are the same. Only I'm a little bit farther in the journey than he is. I hate it for him. I wish he could get answers. More than the answers I can give him.

"Besides, I couldn't let anything happen to you." He finds his fingers very interesting as he says it.

I blink at him a few times, willing him to come into focus more clearly. Why couldn't he let anything happen to me? Because he cared? Because I provide him a way to see my father? Or is it something more?

Gah, I keep asking the same questions and getting zero answers. All I want to know is what's really going on. Is that too much to ask?

Yeah, I have no idea what to say to that. Thankfully, we don't live in silence for long. The door opens and a cheery voice fills the room. "She's awake."

The white blob gets closer to the bed, and only when it's standing next to Abel can I make it out. I'm about ninety-nine percent sure it's a doctor: a lady doctor. She has on a white coat and a jewel-toned purple button-up shirt over black pants. She has on brown glasses, which compliment her red hair beautifully. I think she's very pretty, or at least what I can see of her, which isn't much. Stupid head injury. Stupid ghosts. Imagine, a ghost having that much power to put a girl in the hospital—in a roundabout way anyway.

"Miss Morgan, my name is Doctor Ellis. I'm glad to see you awake."

Her smile is so bright and genuine that I think I could tell her my entire life story, even things I don't want anyone else to know. That's a very dangerous thing. "It's good to be awake," I say and mean it. "Abel said I've been out of it for a while."

Doctor Ellis picks up my chart and flips through it. I wonder if it's to remember me or to kill time. Either way is pretty bad. "You were out a very good while, yes." She flips through a few more pages, probably trying to remember me. That's fine. I don't remember her either. I've never seen her from Adam.

Another person I've never seen before is the nurse that walked in with Doctor Ellis. She has long blond hair that's pulled back in a ponytail. Her scrubs are decorated with fall leaves. She looks like she'd rather be anywhere but here. I feel her pain. She also seems distracted. She takes notes when she's told to, but she's also a million miles away.

"You have a concussion," Doctor Ellis informs me. Like I didn't know that already.

"Despite being out for so long, the tests show that the concussion isn't that bad."

"Not that bad?" Could have totally fooled me. I've been kinda knocked out for the past eight hours. Still, I'm glad I'm fine. It's hard to believe, but it's true.

"No, but I don't want you overexerting yourself. You can still end up in much worse shape, trust me."

I don't know her well enough to trust her.

She keeps right on going. "Take it easy for the next few days. Rest. Relax. You need it. Your body has gone through a terrible ordeal. It needs time to recover.

It hasn't had time to recover in the last six months, why in the world would I give it time now?

"I'm counting on you, young man, to make sure she doesn't overexert herself." She stares Abel right in the eye.

He's not my guardian. He's not anything to me really. I

start to tell her this when Abel, being all awesome and stuff, says, "I'll take care of her. It's all taken care of."

What the what?

"Good," Dr. Ellis says in her firmest voice. I mean, I have no idea if she can get a firmer tone to her voice, but I can't imagine it. It seems pretty rough to me.

My head hurts.

I'm not thinking clearly.

Squirrels.

Nurse Blondie is standing behind the doctor, pretending to take notes. She's not. I squint enough to tell she's on her phone. Texting away by the looks of it. Her eyes are glossy, her jaw tight. Whatever is happening isn't good.

Abel cuts his eyes toward her too ever so briefly. Does he notice it too?

"I mean it, Mister…"

"Hale."

"Mr. Hale. According to our records, Elise has no family we can release her to."

My eyes automatically close as those words echo through my head. No one… I have no one.

"She has me." Abel sounds convincing. If I didn't know better, I'd say he was telling the truth. Unfortunately, I do know better. I know he'll tell the doctor whatever she wants to hear to get me home because that's where he knows I want to be. Then he'll leave and go on his merry way because that's what he thinks I want, and I'll never see him again. Oh, he'll call on occasion to make himself feel better, but ultimately, nope. Never again.

Never.

Again.

I have nobody.

"How long have you dated? No offense intended. However, I need to know how committed you are to taking care of Miss Morgan." Dr. Ellis is a tight ass. Normally, I'd approve. Today, I just want to go home.

I peek through my eyelashes to see what Abel is doing. He crosses his arms, challenging the doctor's stance. Oh good. Here we go. "She has me." Huge emphases on the *me*.

My heart nearly flutters.

I have to keep reminding myself that this is all a complete act. He's good at it, no doubt about that. Still… an act.

He narrows his eyes at the doctor. I'm not sure why. Challenging her, I suppose. When she doesn't back down, he seems a bit put off by it. Well, I'd be put off by it too. And to think I thought she was trustworthy. Turns out, she's a bit of a bitch. Now, don't get me wrong, I appreciate her taking care of me and wanting what's best for me, but right now, he's what's best for me. As hokey as that sounds.

"Fine."

Abel's shoulders relax a little. For the first time, I notice the red on his shirt. It's located mainly on his left shirt sleeve, right at his shoulder. Is he hurt? The doctor doesn't seem to be too concerned about him if he is."

"I'll let her go home, but if you see anything, and I mean anything, out of the ordinary, you bring her in ASAP."

Out of the ordinary like Naked Girl? I smile. I made a funny.

Did they give me pain medicine?

"Do I make myself clear?" Cause Dr. Wonderful has to have the last word on everything.

"Crystal." Abel uncrosses his arms and, to my surprise, grabs my hand. "I'll take care of her."

Now, it could just be my drugged state or the fact that my head feels crazy drunk, but *I'll take care of her* could totally go two ways. One way is… oh yes, I'll take care of her, and she'll be right as rain. And the other way is… you'll never see her again. Unless you check the bottom of the Cumberland River.

I choose to think he's being the kind version and isn't dwelling on the fact that he believes my father killed his entire family.

Yeah, that sort of puts a damper on things.

Nurse Blondie sucks in a breath. She looks scared. Surely it isn't of the doctor, though I can see her as someone who could be difficult to work for.

"I'll get your discharge paperwork filled out. It shouldn't take more than two hours."

"Two?" Abel says what I'm thinking.

"We're a small hospital, Mr. Hale. Not as equip as say Centerville." She makes a point to glare at me when she says Centerville, and at that moment I realize she knows exactly who I am. She knows I'm Roger Morgan's daughter (of course she does, she even said that I didn't have any family), and she knows about Abel. Why would I think she wouldn't?

"You've made your point." It's my time to add to the snarkfest. Might as well not let them have all the fun.

"Good." Period to the end of this stressful conversation. She walks right by the nurse without looking in her direction. For a split second, I think maybe the nurse is a ghost stuck in some sort of an echo.

It would be my luck to have a ghost in the room with me.

When Dr. Ellis shuts the door behind her, Abel lets out a breath and sits down on the bed next to me. His hand is still holding mine. I don't think he notices. I'm not going to tell him. Even though I'm one hundred percent sure there isn't anything between us (on his side anyway), it feels nice to be held. Like in this short moment in time, everything is all right, and I can breathe again. Breathing is good. Comfort and safety is good. Not that I think I have to rely on a man to bring me comfort. Sometimes, though, when everything is a mess, it's nice to feel comfort.

I hope Abel feels the same way about me.

Nurse Blondie looks like she's going to throw up.

"Thank you," I tell Abel. I mean it. Even if this is the last time I'll ever see him, I mean it. He didn't have to stay at the hospital with me. Hell, he could've taken me home like I wanted him to. But he didn't. He stood up for me. I'll never forget it.

"Anytime." He doesn't look at me.

"Hey." I use my free hand, cause I don't want to remind him that he's holding onto mine. "Where did that blood come from?" I touch his shoulder ever so slightly in case it hurts him.

He examines it like it's an afterthought. "It came from you."

From…

I reach up and feel the back of my head.

Oh. My. God.

Sure enough, there are stiches back there. Ugly, thick, painful stitches. "Did they have to shave my head?" Because that's what's important.

He laughs lightly and finally looks at me. "Yes, now you look just like your dad." Then the smile is gone.

I hate talking about my dad too. And I hate that it hurts Abel to talk about my dad. Then again, it would feel weird if it didn't.

"Great." I'd roll my eyes if it didn't hurt. There's a lesson here. Don't unbuckle your seatbelt when you turn around to see two ghosts standing at a graveyard. The more you know…

"No, they didn't shave it. I'm sure your hair will cover it."

"I never want to brush my hair again."

"That'll be attractive."

I'm all done with the banter. I keep touching the back of my head and feeling the stitches. Why… why? "I don't have anyone I have to be attractive for." I'm pouting. Am I really pouting? Yeah, they must've given me some awesome drugs. What happened to the confident, don't-give-a-crap person I used to be? Oh yeah, life screwed her over. Yay.

Bitter much?

"Can we help you?" I let the bitterness out on the one person in the room I don't know. Nurse Blondie, who is still texting. Shouldn't she have moved on by now? Are there no other patients in this hospital?

"I'm sorry. I'm just… I'm sorry." She turns toward the door, and right before she gets to it, she stops. She turns. She comes back. "I'm just… you are Elise Morgan, right? The ghost hunter."

It's a testament to how bad I feel that I don't roll my eyes. Two for two. I deserve a medal. Abel appears to have just noticed that he's holding my hand and abruptly lets it go. Just like that, I'm all alone again.

"She's sick." Abel defends me. "She needs her rest, not to talk to some fan."

Well, there you go.

Nurse Blondie's face turns as red as the blood on Abel's shirt. "Oh, I'm not a fan."

Nice to meet you too.

"I mean…" She's seen the error of her ways. "I mean, I'm not *not* a fan. I watch the show every week. I saw what happened to your family, Mr. Hale. I'm so sorry for your loss."

This lady needs to work on her tact. "So, do you want an autograph or something?"

"Oh, no nothing like that." She clutches her phone and holds it tight against her chest. Her eyes turn shiny. Oh my gosh, I know that look. It's the look mothers get when they're having to do something they don't want to do for their kids. Maybe her kid is a fan?

"Then what?" Abel is showing much more restraint than I am. All I want is to be out of this bed, at my house, and away from people. Is that too much to ask?

"I don't know how to say this without sounding crazy."

"Story of my life." I sigh. "Let's hear it." Come on, lady. Spit it out about how you saw your dead grandmother when you were seven, it's traumatized you every since, and now you want to know if ghosts are real, and what she was trying to say to you.

I'm not sure if I like these drugs or not. On top of bitter, I've become cynical. Though I'm not sure I can completely blame the painkillers for that.

"Well, we moved here a few months ago from Florida. My husband died. I couldn't afford the house, so we sold it and moved up here where the prices for homes aren't as high."

I can feel myself falling asleep, and I don't want that to happen. One, it would be incredibly rude, and two, I feel bad for her. Losing a spouse has to be horrible. My dad never got over losing my mom. Still, I don't see what it has to do with me.

"Did your dead husband follow you up here?" I ask.

Abel's glare tells me to knock it off. Oh honey, I've just started. Someone up my meds, please. I have some things I'd like to get off my chest.

"No, I mean, I don't think so. We moved into a house that needed some renovations. It needed some work, a lot of work actually, and we had the extra money. I thought fixing it up, bringing it back to its old shining glory, would somehow fix me. The work would give me something to do, and making something new would renew me."

It actually makes a lot of sense. My dad did the same after Mom disappeared. He focused on his work, threw himself into it actually, neglecting everyone else around him.

"Did these renovations stir anything up?" Abel asks.

I smack him on the arm. "How do you know what stirs ghosts up?"

"I watch television," he says it with a straight face.

My land, does this man think that ghost hunting is like it is on television? Really? Cause... no.

"Uh-huh. Real ghost hunting isn't like it is on TV." I feel like a snob saying it. I don't care.

"So doing renovations won't stir up spirits?"

"Well, yes it can, but…"

His smirk makes me want to smack him again. Jerk. "Continue with your story," Abel says to Nurse Blondie.

The urge is too strong, and I roll my eyes then. I wish to the Lord I hadn't.

Ouch.

Ouch.

World spinning.

I think I'm going to die.

They don't notice.

If I shut my eyes, it'll stop.

It'll…

Sigh.

It doesn't stop.

"My daughter started seeing things first."

Oh here we go. If I had a dollar for every sob story I've heard that started like that. Actually, most of the time, it's a leaky faucet or a mouse in the attic. Rarely, and I mean rarely, does it turn out to be a ghost. Young girl's imagination plus grieving mom in a new old house is the recipe for a ghost.

The good part of this is that I can lean back with my eyes shut and just listen. Abel can field the questions.

"One night, I heard her talking. It was after three in the morning, and that isn't like her. She's always asleep, always."

"Could it be the new house keeping her up?" I can't keep my mouth shut. Stupid medicine.

"Normally, I'd think that. Except on that night, I heard her talking to the cat."

"Did the cat talk back?" She's going to smack me before long.

"Elise." Abel warns, but I ignore him.

I'll blame the medicine and the concussion if I say something that I regret. Words to live by. Heck yeah, I'm milking this for all it's worth.

"Sorry," I say. I'm not sorry.

"Actually, he did." That makes my eyes open, and I sit up a little straighter. The world isn't spinning so much.

"You're lying." Cause she was.

"I'm not."

I don't say a word. Abel stares at her. She looks at both of us.

Time ticks off from the clock.

"He didn't talk talk, but he answered her in kitty language."

I smack Abel's hand lightly. "In kitty language."

He glares at me. "What else?"

"The next morning when we got up, I asked my daughter, her name is Bethany, what she was doing up so late. She told me it wasn't her. And that she never had a conversation with the cat. That's not the strange part."

"What's the strange part?" Abel is encouraging her.

I need to have a talk with him about his interrogation skills.

"The strange part is that the cat won't stay out at night anymore. He wants to go back in his room. It's like he knows there's something in the house. It's freaky."

"Elise," Abel says my name ever so annoyingly. "You're the expert. Does that sound like something Nurse…?"

"Adams. Julie Adams."

"Nurse Adams should be concerned about?" Abel finished his question.

He's actually asking me to think. Ugh. Okay… "No. She shouldn't be worried. Most likely, your daughter had a nightmare and woke up, chatted with the cat a little, and went back to sleep. She probably doesn't remember any of it. I say you're fine." I glare at Abel. "In my professional opinion."

"Then what about the ghost girl?"

Nurse Julie just had to throw that in there.

"Ghost girl?" Abel is intrigued. Oh good.

"I saw her. Last week, I told Bethany to get in the car because we had to leave. I went into the bathroom to get something I left. When I turned around, I saw Bethany running through the house. Her hair bounced up and down when she ran. And she had yellow ringlets just like Bethany. I yelled for her to go back to the car."

"Let me guess. It wasn't Bethany." Abel winks at me. Oh yeah, he's totally into this.

"It wasn't Bethany. I don't know what it was or where it went, but I know I saw her. Look, I'm not crazy. I know how it sounds, but I'm not crazy. I know what I saw."

This is the part that tugs on my heartstrings. I know what it's like to see something and have no one else believe me. My mom never believed that I saw things. Or I don't think she wanted to believe it. Anytime I did anything strange, my mom sort of freaked out or pretended to ignore me altogether. My dad too. Eventually, I just stopped telling them anything. I might as well if they didn't believe me.

I know it took Nurse Julie Adams a lot of courage to even talk about her story to us, much less to ask for help. I'm assuming that's what she's doing—asking for help.

I drop my attitude and sit up straighter in the bed. It must be her nature because she reaches behind me, without me asking, and fluffs my pillows. I feel awful for every bad and snarky thing I said or thought about her.

"I'm sure you do. I'm not saying you didn't. It's just, in ghost hunting, no matter what you see on television—heck no matter what you saw on *Dark and Deadly Things*—more often than not, the so-called paranormal activity can be explained. A house settling. An electrical issue. Mice. Something else that can cause panic, and it's perfectly normal to panic, especially after all you've been through."

"I'm not panicking." She tries to keep going.

Abel cuts her off. "We know you aren't."

We do?

"I know this has to be scary for you. I know what it's like to think there might be something in your house, but you aren't sure. And you have no idea where to turn."

Julie Adams to admitting. Julie Adams to admitting, comes over the intercom again.

"I've been here too long. I'll probably get in trouble. I don't care. I have to know if this is something I should worry about. That was my daughter texting me. She's home with the babysitter and scared to death."

It's normal for a child to miss her mother and do anything to get her home. I don't think that's paranormal. The girl with the bouncy hair, though. That's very interesting. It's something I can't explain offhand.

"We can come check it out for you, if you want," Abel says almost too giddily.

"We can?"

He cuts his eyes at me with a silent, "Zip it."

"You don't have to do that. I know you're hurt, and Mr. Hale, your family… I can't imagine. I didn't mean you had to come to my house. I just wanted to know if I should worry about this. But if you think there's nothing to be afraid of, I'll tell Bethany—"

"We'll be there." Abel gives his definitive answer.

"We will?" I'm sure he'd rather I shut up.

"Give us your address. What time do you get off?"

Abel is an eager little beaver, ain't he?

Nurse Julie shakes her head. "You don't have to come tonight. It's very kind of you, but I think it was a mistake asking you."

She starts to walk away, and Abel jumps up and blocks her. "Because of Elise? Don't worry about her. She's a bit moody."

"I'm not moody."

I'm so moody.

"She's had a bit of a rough day and, you know, pain

medicine and all. She'll be her normal cheery self in no time."
Abel beams at Julie.

I'll show him my cheery self.

"No, I don't want to trouble you guys. Like I said, I never should've asked about it."

"When your child is scared, you'd do anything," Abel reminds her.

"True."

"Then tell us a good time, and we'll be there."

"Ummm… well, I don't want it to be too soon so Elise can get over her injury."

"I'm fine." I remind everyone in the room while my head hates me. "Don't worry about me."

"See, she's fine. Do you work tomorrow?"

Abel is like an overexcited kid in a candy store. I have no idea why. I didn't think ghost hunting was his thing. And if it was his thing, I figured he'd be looking for them in his house, not in someone else's.

Nurse Julie shakes her head. "Not tomorrow."

"Good, can you take Bethany out for a late movie? Elise, doesn't it need to be dark for us to investigate?"

Another thing everyone thinks now thanks to all the ghost-hunting shows. Oh joy. "Not necessarily. Is there any time the supposed activity strikes up?"

Supposed activity. That'll win me brownie points with her.

"Um… three at night. And sometimes during the day."

"So no real pattern."

She shakes her head.

"Okay." Abel looks at me. "Can we go around four and stay as long as we need to? Do you have any of your dad's hunting equipment?"

I wish he wouldn't mention my dad. "No." It's as much of an answer as I want to give. I hope he gets my stop-talking-about-it tone.

"No, you don't have any, or you don't have your dad's?"

Son of a bitch. "I have my own."

"Excellent." He bites back and turns his kilowatt smile toward Nurse Julie. "Is four okay with you? Can you be out of the house for a few hours? Oh! An even better idea! What time do you get off today? We can swing by your house on the way to take Elise home."

She looks at me with pity, like she feels bad she even brought it up. "Shouldn't you go home and get things… rest."

I wonder if she thinks Abel is as crazy as I do because of the head trauma and all. I think I should at least go home and change clothes before I go off and fight ghosts. Seems logical to me. Maybe not to anyone else.

"We can rest later," Abel so helpfully adds. "And we'll swing by and get the stuff we need on the way. I know you want to help your daughter. Let's say we meet you at your house later tonight? Would that give you plenty of time?"

"Yes." She nods. "I think so. But does it give you enough time?"

Abel tilts his head slightly. If I did that, the room would never stop spinning. "As long as you get us discharged really fast we can."

Julie looks from Abel to me. I'm sure I look as marvelous as I feel. "Are you sure about this, Miss Morgan?"

No.

"Yes. I'm definitely sure. If something is scaring your daughter, then we need to figure out what it is. No little girl should be scared like that. Ever."

Then it hits me why Abel is so adamant about this. His sister was scared. No one believed her. Her parents brought in *Dark and Deadly Things,* and we all know how that ended. He's scared that will happen again to another family.

Nurse Julie smiles brightly, writes something down on a piece of paper she had in her pocket, and hands it to Abel. Then she tucks her clipboard under her arm and takes Abel by the hands. "Thank you. Thank you so much!"

"You're welcome." He smiles back.

I regret all of this already.

I feel bad for Nurse Julie, I do. I feel bad for her daughter as well. Still, I haven't hunted for ghosts in about six months, and it's never been hard for me cause, I mean, I see them. This should be an open and shut case.

Course, it should be a case that wasn't opened in the first place.

Julie Adams to the admitting station now. Julie Adams.

Someone is getting annoyed other than me. I bet ole Dr. Ellis is causing a ruckus cause her right hand woman isn't there.

"I should go. Thank you. I'll see you in a few hours." She smiles and then leaves.

I clear my throat as Abel tucks the address in his pocket. "What was that all about?"

"She needs help. We can help."

"I can help. I can walk in that house and, in ten minutes at the most, tell her if it's haunted, and I guarantee you it isn't."

"Wanna make a friendly bet?"

"No."

"Chicken. Bock, bock."

I glare.

"If you're so all-fired sure the house isn't haunted, then prove it. If you're right and there aren't any ghosts there, then I'll come to your dorm and feed you supper one night."

"That's… weird." I snicker. Weird, but at least it'll keep him around a little longer. I wouldn't hate that, even if he is annoying. "And if you win, which you won't, but *if* you did?"

He takes time to contemplate this. His eyes widen, and the light bulb goes off in his brain. He walks toward me slowly and doesn't stop until he's sitting on the side of my bed. This could either be really really good or really really bad.

"If I win, you go with me to my house."

"Your house?"

"My house. The one your dad investigated. You come with me, and you find out what the hell happened to my family."

I can hear my heart monitor speed up. I don't want to go back there. As much as I'd love to find out what happened, I don't want to go to that house. It's one thing seeing the ghost of my mom. It's another to see whatever that black mass was.

Abel sticks his hand out toward me. His eyes are steely blue, challenging me. "Do we have a deal, Elise?"

CHAPTER FOURTEEN

I HATE HIM.

I hate him and his stupid car.

I hate everything about him.

I hate the fact that he took me to the hospital and stayed with me.

I hate that he's driving me home.

I hate that I shook his stupid hand. Now, if there is a ghost at the Adams's house, then I have to go to his and come face to face with whatever thing is in there.

I hate a lot of things right now.

Mostly I hate that my freakin' pain medicine has worn off, and I don't want to take anymore until I get home. Ghost hunting while on pain pills isn't the smartest idea ever. No telling what I'll see in that house while high on prescription drugs. Lord help me.

"We'll swing by my hotel room first so I can grab a shirt." He hasn't stopped talking since I was released from the hospital. I haven't said a word. I don't know if this is nervous talking or his normal self, but I wish he'd stop. My head hurts. And, frankly, I don't want to hear it.

I'm mad enough that I agreed to do this.

"Then we need to swing by your place and get your equipment. Is it in your dorm or at your parent's house?"

I so don't want to answer him.

He sighs. "I know you don't want to do this, okay? I get it. I do. You don't feel good. We saw your father. Things are weird, and you don't know if they'll ever get better. I get it, all right? I do. But I'm not letting this little girl worry another second longer than she should. If there's nothing there, great, good. We'll leave, and she can have peace of mind."

Would she have peace of mind or would Abel?

"But if there's something there, they need to know so they can get out. They need help like my parents needed help, and I'm not going to let this family down like..."

He stops mid-sentence. I know what he's trying to say. "You don't want to let your family down like my father let you down."

His hands grip the wheel tighter. It feels like a huge weight is on my shoulders, holding me down. It's on my shoulders and on my chest. Anxiety is threatening to take over again. I can't have that happen.

I think I'm going to cry.

I blame the pain medicine for that too.

"I don't blame your father. I don't. Not really."

"Could have fooled me. How you went after him at the hospital."

"I know. I'm sorry about that. I just need answers. That's why I need to go back to my house."

"You haven't been at all?"

"The police still have it taped off as a crime scene. I don't know what they're waiting for. It isn't like evidence is going to jump up at them now. I heard it might be in the next day or two that they let me go home."

"Do you think you can? Go home I mean." There goes my vow to never talk to him again.

"It'll never be home. Not now. But I do need to go there. Find whatever hurt my family."

"And then what?"

His nose flares. "Kill it."

CHAPTER FIFTEEN

I LET THOSE TWO LITTLE WORDS run through my mind as he runs into his hotel room and changes clothes. I don't go in with him. I figure he needs some time to himself. I do too, truth be told.

He wants to kill whatever is in his house. He wants to kill the thing that killed his parents and his little sister, and I get it. I totally do. I wanted to go after the thing that killed my mom when it happened. I couldn't though. How do you kill something that's already dead?

This is what makes ghost hunting so much more difficult than say real hunting. You can find a deer or a squirrel and make a meal out of it. You can shoot it, stuff it, hang it on your mantle. But, as far as I know, there is no way to kill a ghost. Ghosts are sort of ghosts for a reason—there isn't a way to get rid of them.

If there were, I'd love to know how it worked. I'd love to help the ghosts I see move on to the other side. If I could get my mother to move on, I'd be a content lady.

I don't know how.

And if Abel thinks I do, then he has another think

coming.

There are other paranormal shows on television that build traps to catch ghosts. I'm not sure if they work. I've never seen any evidence that they do. I do know the thing that killed his family, if it's the same type of thing that went after my mom, is much more powerful than a regular ordinary ghost. No small little trap or spell is going to get rid of it.

That freaks me out too.

My phone vibrates in my pants. The hospital was nice enough to let me have some scrub pants. I'm sure they'll show up on the bill. I pull it out and look at the name. Silas Ford is texting me… again.

I should've probably called him and told him I was in the hospital. Then he'd come and there would've been even more of a ruckus. It wasn't worth it.

I'm sure I've been on the news. I don't see any photographers around right now, but I'm sure they're lurking somewhere. You don't have Abel Hale and Elise Morgan together and not have a photo or two.

My dad's warning echoes through my head. He told me not to trust Silas. Course, my dad is also certifiably crazy. So there's that.

I decide to read the text. Abel is taking forever to change. Maybe he took a shower or something. There was a lot of blood, and it probably soaked through his shirt.

Where are you? Heard you were in an accident. Not at hospital. Seen you on the news with Abel Hale. What's going on? Call me!

Guess it hasn't crossed his mind that he can call me.

I'm sure he knows I wouldn't answer. He's my ex-boyfriend for a reason.

I'm fine. Small accident. Few stitches. I'll live. Abel wanted to see Dad. That's it.

I press send and lay my head back against the headrest. A nap would be nice. A nap and my bed at home. Naked Girl staring at me while she tries to tell me something. Normal things. I hope this case doesn't take long. I've got all the things to do… like rest.

The bottle of pain pills the doctor gave me before I left is calling my name. I have to fight the urge, though, because I ain't going in that house full of pills. It's freaky enough to see dead people. More freaky to do it on drugs.

I know that for a fact.

Why are you with him? E, you need me to come and get you? Where are you? We need to talk.

Silas won't stop.

Leave me alone. Where were you the last two weeks when I might have needed you?

Ex-girlfriend burn. He shouldn't mess with me. I'm in a mood.

This isn't a relationship thing, Elise! Stop acting like a child. It's much more than that. I might know what attacked Abel's family. I had the network pull the tapes.

My blood runs ice cold.

You saw it?

He writes back: *I saw it.*

"Ready?"

I didn't hear Abel open the car door or slide in. At the sound of his voice, I jump like I've been shot or like I'm really guilty. I turn off my phone and hold it in my hands.

"Uh, Elise? Everything okay?"

Abel looks nice. I have to admit. He has on jeans and a black short-sleeved shirt. It's still way too hot in Tennessee for November. His hair is wet, falling almost into his eyes. So I was right. He did take a shower.

"Everything's fine." I lie… again. And feel my phone vibrating in my hand. Yet another lie that I've told Abel about things he probably should know about. I'm a horrible person. I'll tell him everything when I know what to say.

He narrows his eyes. "Then why do you look guilty?"

"You don't know me well enough to know when I look

guilty."

"You aren't that hard to read." He starts the car and pulls into drive.

"I am so. My mind is like Fort Knox."

"Right... I just happened to know that you can see ghosts because your mind is Fort Knox." He pulls away from the hotel and onto the main road. "Do you need to go by your dorm and get some clothes?"

"No, when I go to my dorm, I'm staying there for a good forever."

"Never leaving?"

"Never. I'm staying there until the second coming of the Lord. Or until the food runs out. Whichever comes first."

He laughs, making his dimple shine. I like it when his dimple shines. "At least you have your priorities."

Time to backtrack. "I never should have told you that I can see ghosts. It was... something I try to keep to myself. People look at you strange. Do you believe that I can see them?"

"Guess I'll find out at the Adam's house, won't I?"

My phone is going to vibrate my hand off. I hope Abel can't hear it. I think Silas is calling me. I think he can lump it. "So, why are you so interested in the Adams house?"

He shrugs. "She needs help. We can help her, I told you that."

"I think there's more to it." My phone vibrates again. Shut up, Silas.

"And if I'm right, I get you to my house. I want you at my house."

"Ah, if I had a nickel for every guy who tells me that." I wink in his direction. Actually, if I had a nickel for every guy who asked me to his house, I'd have one nickel. I didn't even go home with Silas. Guess I wasn't good enough for him to introduce me to his family. He mentioned it. We had actually talked about it. Then my mom died, and well, things sort of went under.

"I don't mean like that."

Twist the knife, why don't you? I know he doesn't want me like that, but can't he let a girl daydream? It's all I have left at the moment. "I know you don't."

"I just…" He glances in my direction. "I don't mean I wouldn't think of you like that. Any guy would. You are—"

"Smart and funny and blah blah blah." I answer for him. I don't like being so bitter. I totally blame the medicine even though it isn't in my system anymore.

"Oh stop it. Like you don't know how beautiful you are." I think he's sincere. Does the man not have eyes?

"I think there's more to life than looks, says the girl sitting here in borrowed hospital scrubs."

"I think they'll make you pay for them now."

"Oh, I'm sure it's already on the bill."

Abel sighs. "I didn't mean any offense, okay. I'm just saying that I need you to come to my house and see what's there. A bet seemed the best way to get you there."

"Asking seemed out of the question?"

"I think I did ask you. And I think you said no."

Well there's that. I point to my head. "Concussion. I don't remember everything." I'll use that excuse until the day I die if I have to. I like it. I hate the pain, but head trauma sure is handy to blame everything on.

"Uh-huh. Sure. Well, now it's a bet, and a bet is a bet. So there." He turns onto Stone Mountain Road.

"So when I'm right, and there isn't a ghost there, you won't hound me to go to your house?" Hound isn't a nice word. I think it fits this situation though.

"I don't hound you."

I stare at him.

"Okay, I do. It's for a good cause, though."

Whatever.

"And what makes you so sure there isn't anything in that

house. Nurse Julie saw something. Seems like you of all people would believe it."

That's a low blow. "Just because I can see things doesn't mean that I believe everyone who says that they do."

"What about me?" His question certainly throws me for a loop.

"What about you what?"

"What if I told you I had powers? Would you believe me?"

"Do you?"

"Would you?"

That's an interesting question. "I doubt it. I've never met anyone who can do things like me." My phone buzzes again. At this rate, all my battery life will be gone. Damn phone. Damn Silas Ford.

"That you know of." His comebacks are getting on my nerves.

"I suppose so."

"You've met Julie, and she claims to have seen a ghost. How is that not like you?"

Oh for the love of Pete.

"It is and you know it. Stop being like this."

"Like what?"

"Annoying." If Silas Ford doesn't stop texting my phone... I can't deal with him on top of Abel. It's not right.

"You didn't think I was annoying when I got in the car and you checked out my ass."

I... have no words for that. "I've found through this car ride that you are an even bigger ass than your derrière."

Boom. Drops mic.

I'm done.

He slows down and turns on his blinker. Soon we're turning past a mailbox painted like a little red barn and up the narrow driveway to Julie's house. It's a bit of a long driveway, where driveways are concerned. It dips and goes back up a hill and then to the left. Then, I finally see the house.

Julie Adams wasn't lying. This house is old.

It reminds me of the old plantation house in *Gone with the Wind*. Well, maybe not as immaculate as Tara, but it definitely has it's stateliness.

"Whoa!" I say as I sit up so I can look out the window. "That place is beautiful."

"Tell me there's no ghost in there. It's straight out of *Scooby Doo*."

If he gets his ghost hunting ability from Scooby, then we're doomed. "You know there never were any real ghosts on *Scooby Doo*. They were all just people in costumes. By that logic, I should win this bet easily."

"Don't count on it. If there's any place that's haunted, it's this house."

He's not wrong in the description of it. It's a two-story white house with four wide columns connecting the roof to the large porch outside. There's a balcony on the second floor, overlooking the driveway. I wonder who lived here before. Why did they move? And who originally built it?

There is a black Honda in the driveway. Probably Julie's.

"Ready for this?" he asks, not taking his eyes off the rather impressive and in dire-need-of-an-outside-renovation house.

"As ready as I'm going to be."

"You sure you don't need any equipment? We can still go back and get it."

I shake my head, clutching my phone tighter. "The only equipment I need to see ghosts are these." I point to my eyes.

"What if it tries to talk to us? Can you hear it?"

"There isn't—"

"A ghost. I know. Humor me. Can you hear it?"

"No." I wish to God that I could.

"That's sad."

That's an understatement. "It is."

"What about an EVP thingy. Can you hear ghosts on that?"

I just blink at him.

"Okay then, I'm ready for you to be proven wrong." He smiles as he opens his door and gets out.

I don't immediately follow him. I take the few seconds to check my phone. Silas has sent me seventeen text messages. And this is one reason why we broke up. The last message is the only one I read.

Stop ignoring me! I have the tape from the network. There's something you need to see. Meet me at your house—your grandma's house—Friday at seven. I'll show you then and get your take on it. K?

People who can't even take the effort to type an O in front of that K drive me up the wall.

He gives me a strange predicament, though. Friday is the day after tomorrow. I could see the black mass. I could see what Silas has up his sleeves. If I'm to trust my dad, I shouldn't have anything to do with Silas. Then again, when have I ever listened to my dad?

Works for me. See you then. I push send and get out of the car.

This house is foreboding, but it isn't haunted.

I'd stake my life on that.

CHAPTER SIXTEEN

"ARE YOU COMING?" ABEL IS A bit of the impatient type. The kind that wants to get the show on the road.

I'm impatient too, but about important things like Netflix or the time it takes a pizza to cook.

I shove my phone back in my pocket and get out of the car. A chilly wind hits me immediately, and I shiver. I don't think I've shivered all of November so far. It's kinda nice to feel the cool wind.

"Feel that?" I ask Abel, who is looking up at the house with a bit of trepidation. I bet he's nervous. Can't say I blame him. The last time he was in a supposedly haunted house, it didn't end well for him.

Doesn't mean I can't have a little fun with him, though.

The medicine... I totally blame the medicine.

"Feel what?"

"The cold."

"It's the wind." I'm not sure if even he believes it.

"It's not all the wind. When we investigate houses and there's a strong cold presence, it is very telling."

"It is?" He turns my direction, and I can see it written all over his face. He's interested.

Well boy howdy.

"It is."

"What is it telling of?"

I sigh and walk by him, taking care to barely graze my arm against his. "That it's cold outside."

Boom.

Drops mic.

Walks away.

"Har." He deadpans behind me as I start up the steps to, and even I have to admit it, a really creepy house. "You're hilarious."

"It's the medicine."

"Or the concussion."

"Who knows? I'm normally much funnier." I wink at him, and I can feel my face turning all kinds of red.

What did I do?

Wink?

Really?

Have I started hitting on people now? Flirting?

Please tell me I'm not flirting with Abel Hale because I know in my heart of hearts that would end badly. It isn't that I don't want to flirt with him. I totally do. I want him to be interested in me. I want him to see me as someone other than Roger Morgan's daughter.

Except I know that's all I am to him. It's all I'll ever be to him. And that's all I can expect.

"I imagine you're very different when you are yourself." He stands next to me, and I have to fight myself to look up at him. His hands are behind his back, his eyes are focused on the door, and he's not cracked a smile.

I know concussions and medicine can mess with your emotions. I know that. Doesn't mean that when it's your emotions being messed with that it doesn't hurt any less. I've done this to myself.

"I wish you could get to know me then. The real me." I hear the sadness in my voice. The aching. The, God help me, longing. I hate feeling like this, vulnerable. I don't need anyone. Which is good because I have no one.

Abel looks at me then. He bites his lip, and I swear there's something he wants to say to me. I want him to say it. I lean in to hear the words. Good or bad, I don't care. I just need him to say something.

I wonder how long I can blame the medicine on this.

The door opens just like in every crappy soap opera on the planet, and Julie Adams steps outside. She's still in her scrubs from the hospital, only now her hair is down and she has a touch of fresh lipstick on her lips.

She walks past us and motions for us to follow.

We do and end up next to the car. "Thank you for coming out here today. You didn't have to."

She motions toward my head, my head that's killing me. "I'm fine." I'll be fine someday. I have high hopes of that.

"Why are we out here instead of talking inside?" Abel asks.

I keep reminding myself that Abel has never actually been an investigator on an investigation. He's only seen what happens on television. Before *Dark and Deadly Things* got picked up, my parents and I went to lots of different houses, and in every one that had kids, the parents wanted to talk to us outside. It's funny, the kids are normally the ones who see the paranormal activity first, but it's the parents who try to keep their children from knowing what's going on. To protect them…

In my experience, the paranormal don't care if you're a child or an adult. They'll make contact with you no matter what if they have something to say.

"She doesn't want her daughter to hear." I'd slap him upside the head to make my point if I were closer. No, I wouldn't. I don't think I'm that mean, but the thought would cross my mind.

"Ah... okay." He turns to me and raises a brow like he thought her daughter already knew, and I nod because I can understand his non-verbal cues. We both turn back toward Julie. "What exactly do we need to know before we go in? Has something else happened today?"

Julie scoffs and pulls out a cigarette. She lights it up right in front of us, God, and everybody. "Actually, I don't want Bethany, that's my daughter, to know I've started smoking again."

She takes a big draw, savoring every particle of nicotine. "And to answer your question, Mr. Hale—"

"Abel." He corrects.

"Abel. To answer your question, something happens every day. So the fact that something happened isn't unusual."

"Then what *is* unusual?" I ask, trying to move this along.

"Bethany said today the ghost stood and stared at her."

I've heard a lot of stories in my twenty-one years, been on a lot of investigations. Not many things freak me out anymore—well, what happened in Abel's house freaked me out—but normal paranormal things don't. What Julie said, though, gives me goosebumps, and I'm not sure why.

Maybe because I know that if there's a ghost here, then I have to go to Abel's house and investigate as per our bet. I don't want to go to Abel's house and investigate. I'm terrified of what I'll find there, or what will find us. I have my reasons.

"She s-s-stared at her." I stutter out the word *stared*. Abel notices. Of course he would.

She takes another draw of her cigarette. "Yeah, it freaked her out because she said she, my daughter, tried to talk to the ghost, and she didn't do anything. Just stared at her. Bethany said she was about her size and has blond curls, like the girl I saw out of the corner of my eye."

My hands start shaking. I don't know why. I've done this way too many times. This is a milk run for people like me.

This is something I could do in my sleep if I wanted. It's a scared girl with probably some form of lower-level ghost in her house. Nothing to be afraid of.

Except I am afraid.

I can feel my heart rate speed up.

My heart is beating superfast.

I do everything in my power not to let Julie or Abel know. Especially not Abel. I'm the professional here, and he's the first timer. He should be the one that's scared to death, not me.

I don't know what's going on with me lately, but I don't like it.

I think it's seeing my mom.

That does a number on you.

My mom as a ghost. My dad in a mental ward.

I can't handle all of this on top of the pounding headache.

Add to that, I can relate to Bethany. I remember being very little, much too little to know that I should keep my mouth shut and not tell anyone about the ghosts I saw. And no one would believe me. I want to believe her. I want to win my bet with Abel.

I want world peace.

I want to go to sleep...

"Can we talk to your daughter?" Abel asks.

Julie will say no. In these situations, they always say no. "I'd rather you not. She doesn't know why you are here. I prefer if she doesn't."

"You don't want her to know you believe her." I think Julie believes her more than Abel does.

"I don't want her to be any more scared than she already is." She taps her cigarette. Ashes fall to the ground. "I hadn't smoked in about ten years until my husband died. Suicide actually."

I flinch. God, suicides are brutal.

"Bethany never got over it."

I don't see how anybody could.

A tear slides down Julie's cheek. Such a heartbreaking story. "Bethany loved her father. That love was part of the reason I stayed when we argued." She looks from Abel to me and smiles sadly. "You two are young, but there will come a time when no matter how much you love someone, you'll want out. It's just the way of life. Sometimes you stay and work it out. Sometimes you don't."

"Did she start seeing ghosts after that?" I ask. I know she didn't. I remember from what Julie told us in the hospital that Bethany didn't see them until she moved here. Heck, by the looks of this rundown, way past fixer-upper, there's no way anyone wouldn't see ghosts here. It's freaky as hell. In fact, it would make Edgar Alan Poe nervous.

"Not until we got here. I saw this house, and I thought I could bring it to life again."

I don't even think Dr. Frankenstein could bring this house back.

"I know what you're thinking." She drops the cigarette to the ground and steps on it. "You're thinking that I have to be an idiot to have bought this house."

"I didn't say that."

"You don't have to, Miss Morgan." She smiles sadly. "Truth be told, I was a bit of an idiot. I bit off more than I could chew. Thought the renovation would give me something to do, keep my mind off missing my husband. I do miss him, you know. Even after all the crap, all the fights. I miss how he was when we first got married. I've brought her away from her home to live here where she sees ghosts and is scared all the time. What kind of a mother am I?"

Abel, to my surprise, wraps his arms around her and allows her to cry on his shoulder. He rubs her back in gentle circles as the nurse he just met a few hours ago bawls on his shoulder like she's known him her entire life.

I wonder if he has that effect on all people. I know sometimes I feel like I could fall into his arms and cry too. Or kiss him.

Whichever.

While Able is comforting Julie, I turn around and survey the house. It's... well, it's old. Quaint would be giving quaint a bad name. The upstairs windows are tall and skinny. I see a curtain move in the middle one. Bethany catching a glimpse of us, no doubt. I wonder what she thinks about all this? Mostly, and I hate to think this because I've been in her shoes, I know what it's like to see things no one else can see and have no one believe her. But, even with that, I have to put that aside and wonder how much of this is truly a child's imagination. She misses her father. Her mother pulled Bethany from the only place she's ever lived, away from her friends.

Her mother moved Bethany *here*.

What if the child simply wants to go home and is making up this ghost stuff to play on her mom's emotions so she'll sell the house and move back home?

I wouldn't put it past any child.

And I wouldn't fault her for it either.

It's a rather smart plan, actually. "How old is Bethany?" I ask when Julie finally releases Abel and wipes her eyes.

"She's eight. She turned eight in July."

"Okay," I walk up to her and take her hands. She doesn't fall into my arms or on my shoulder like she did Abel. I must be losing my touch. Then again, from what I've seen, anyone could feel inferior when they deal with Abel in the emotional department. That man has his stuff together.

Especially for someone who buried his family yesterday.

"We need you to go inside and get Bethany. Take her out for maybe four or five hours. When you come back, we'll have some news for you."

She nods and takes a deep breath. "Do you think the house is really haunted? Do you think it's something we should be afraid of? Because I know on your show your dad always tells people he doesn't see any malicious intent."

"In my experience" — Abel's nose flares — "sometimes that isn't the case."

CHAPTER SEVENTEEN

JULIE AND BETHANY ARE GONE TWENTY minutes later. Julie introduced us to Bethany, much to my surprise. I figured Julie wouldn't want her daughter to know we were there. Bethany seemed excited to meet us. She gave me a hug and told me not to go into the second room upstairs. That's where I saw the curtain move.

Oh good.

The sun is very low in the sky when they pull out of the driveway. Abel and I stand shoulder to shoulder—or elbow to shoulder in our case—and look up at the empty, imposing structure.

"So, you really think it isn't haunted?" he teases.

"Guess we'll find out soon enough." I sigh. I hope to God I'm not wrong, and it's just a child wanting to go home, saying anything to make it happen. I don't want to see a ghost. I don't want to lose our bet. I don't want to go to that house with Abel.

But here I am.

All concussed and all, fixing to go inside this house.

Why do these things happen to me?

"Ready?" he asks without giving me time to say yay or nay.

I follow him up the creaking steps. The wooden porch swing, with the white paint dangling from it in small flakes, squeaks in the breeze. I hate houses like this... well, I take that back. I love houses like this, in pictures. I like driving by them and taking pictures of them. I like to post them on Instagram and like them on Facebook. However, I don't like going inside them.

Most people who hunt ghosts say they aren't afraid of the supernatural.

I'm not afraid of it, normally.

But I'm terrified today.

I haven't been ghost hunting since the incident, and I swore I never would again.

Here I am.

Abel puts his hand on the door and, after a second's hesitation, pushes it open.

He looks at me.

I look at him.

"Ladies first?"

I glare at him, and in an attempt to prove to him that this doesn't bother me, I step inside.

Normally on television, they turn the lights off when we do these types of investigations. It's all night vision and thermal cameras and all that stuff that looks cool on television but isn't really necessary. Not when you can see ghosts anyway.

"Want the lights off?" Abel asks from the doorway with his hand over the switch.

"What would we see with?"

He holds up a small pocket flashlight.

"Why walk around in the dark when Julie and Bethany see the ghost in the light?"

He shrugs. "I don't know. This is sort of my first rodeo."

"Well, it ain't mine." I sound bitter. I am bitter.

"Sorry." He sighs and comes to where I am in the entryway. I have to admit this house is really pretty. Much prettier on the inside than it is on the outside. When you first walk in, there's a grand staircase that curves up to the second floor. How people did that way back in the day when this house was built, I have no idea. But it is beautiful. To my left, it looks like a parlor of some kind. An outside door is in front of me. A dining room is to my right.

"It's pretty in here." He's making small talk. I take that to mean he's nervous. His last adventure with a ghost didn't end well for him either. We're a fine pair to be here.

"It is."

"Do you see anything?"

It would be easy if something just jumped out and went boo, wouldn't it? Well, it would make it easier on me anyway. I don't like having to look for them. It's a game of hide and seek that no one wins. The ghost gets found, and I get jump scared (normally) out of my mind.

"Nothing." I'm a bit sad about that. My head is killing me. I want to go home, and I know I won't get to until I find something. I don't see Abel giving up until Julie and Bethany get home, unless we find something. He's determined to get me to his house.

I won't tell him that even if we do find something here, I might not go to Hale House. He can hate me all he wants. It all depends on what Silas shows me tomorrow. If it's something scary—and I mean possess-me-if-I-let-it scary—then hell no. I'm not going anywhere near that.

I take a step.

Abel takes a step.

The floorboards creak upstairs.

Crap.

"Did you hear that?" he whispers, grabbing my arm.

"Scared?" I smile. I shouldn't kid about something like

this. He has every right to be terrified of the paranormal. But this is how I cope with things. I freak out on the inside and hide behind sarcasm on the outside.

He looks down and sees his hand grabbed onto mine. He quickly releases me, much to my chagrin. "No. I'm not scared."

"Uh-huh." I roll my eyes and instantly regret it. Concussions are horrible things.

Horrible.

Horrible things.

The stairs creak as I step on the bottom one. Abel flinches beside me. "That was me." I'm partly kidding, partly reassuring. It's just me. It's okay. We haven't gotten to the scary part yet.

That'll be waiting for us on the second floor.

There's running upstairs. He pulls on my arm to stop me. Please tell me this isn't going to be how this goes all night. If it is, we're never going to get done. The point of being a ghost hunter is to hunt ghosts. If we run or jump or flinch every time we see or hear something, that makes us slow and unprofessional.

Two things I never want to be.

He points up to the second floor. His eyes are wide, and I think he might be having a nervous breakdown. "A mouse, you think?"

I shake my head. Oh, poor little innocent Abel Hale. "Not a mouse." I mouth the words as I shake his hand off me and head up to the second floor.

Whatever's in this house, and I guess I'll have to accept that there's something here now, begrudgingly, is either running off to hide or... and I won't tell Abel this, luring us somewhere. There have been cases where the ghost wanted me to find something: one time a locket, another a gun. If that's the case with this ghost, then we have an intelligent haunting, and those are freaky as heck. I can't imagine my soul floating around without a body. That's exactly what it's like to be a ghost. Just hanging around. Nowhere to go. And if it knows what it's doing... those are so sad.

"Something's upstairs," Abel says helpfully.

I nod because I'm not a total bitch, and we continue on our trek up the curved stairs.

Once we get to the top, the last orange rays from the setting sun are shining through the bedroom windows, saying goodbye to the day and welcoming night. I don't hate the dark, but I also know what sorts of things can be in it: things I don't ever want to see again.

The footsteps have stopped for now. That means we have to go to every room and search every closet and behind every curtain, and I don't have time for that.

I have a bed that needs me, and a headache that is threatening to take lives, namely mine.

"I'll check this room. You check that one." I'll take the one that had the moving curtain earlier. It occurs to me that it might not have been Bethany looking out. Ghosts are naturally curious sorts—curious and I'm sure bored out of their mind—so they sometimes can be seen looking out of windows. That's good for me.

Abel nods and heads toward the first door on the left, which I believe is a bedroom. He doesn't have any equipment or anything normal people use to hunt ghosts with. All he has are his normal eyes and his normal body. I'm sort of sending him on a get-out-of-my-way mission. I need my space, and he'd be crowding it.

With him gone, I open the door to the bedroom and suck in my breath. If I see something, what am I going to do? Run? This has been one of my main problems with ghost hunting since the beginning. We tell ghosts we can help them. We tell them we're going to move them to a better place or let them move on. But in the end, all we do is disturb them, make them upset to get proof that they're there, and then leave. That seems inhumane to me, well as inhumane as you can treat a ghost. Of course, ghosts were once people too and deserve respect.

Some of my colleagues, Silas Ford among them, didn't think the same things as me. Ghosts were cows to lead to the slaughter. Nothing more than things to make money on, to hell with their feelings.

People who think that get on my ever-loving nerves.

I don't ever want to be like that as long as I live.

"See anything!" Abel yells from across the hall so loud I jump. That idiot.

I stick my head out the door. "Don't be so loud. You'll scare her off," I gripe.

"What if she scares me off first?" He smiles at me from the doorway of the room he's supposed to be inspecting.

"Then I suppose you'll totally miss the incredible ghost/hunter threesome, ya think?"

His face tinges red, and I smile brighter. There might be a young human in this old dude somewhere. "You'd have to be involved for it to be a threesome."

I just let that little comment hang in the air. He's not flirting. He doesn't care. I don't care. It's business, and nothing more.

Nothing more.

So why can't I wipe this stupid grin off my face.

The sun has almost set, and I pull out a small flashlight from my bag. Yeah, I could turn on the room light, but old ghost-hunting rituals take over sometimes. This room is impressive. Not by the furnishings, which are scarce I might add. I think this might be like a spare room or a catch-all. It's impressive with all the details on the ceiling, especially the crown molding, which seems to be in pretty good shape considering the age and decay of the rest of the house. It looks like this might have been a reading room or a second parlor. I don't imagine it was a bedroom, though it might have been. I never paid that much attention to our investigations—not the history part anyway.

The walls are covered with a hunter-green-and-gold wallpaper. Some would call it gaudy. I'd call it beautiful. The green is the background, and the gold is laid out in a flower pattern in vertical stripes down the wall. I bet that was hard to lay straight. Pieces of it are falling off the walls. One is torn nearly in half.

I try to picture what happened in this room all those years ago. Is the wallpaper falling apart because of time, or is Julie trying to take it off and renovate the space? I would leave the wallpaper, truth be told. It gives the room character.

The door behind me slams shut. I jump and drop my flashlight on the ground. Damn, I've become a cliché.

Footsteps. I hear them, and I'm totally not happy about it. They aren't mine, and they are too light for Abel.

I don't care if someone sees ghosts every day of their life, it can still be unnerving if they aren't really expecting it.

"Hello? Where are you?" I kneel down to grab my flashlight, which is still on and shining toward the window. My fingers are trembling and uncooperative. When I find the flashlight, I accidently push it forward.

I'm hopeless.

It goes closer to the curtains. I really don't want to go over there. "Who's here with me?" I ask into the darkness, not like I could really hear an answer.

I can't see a thing, which means I can't see her either.

Why couldn't I have come into this room when the sun was out? Why didn't I turn on a light? So many questions. I think I like giving myself obstacles to overcome. Keeps me grounded.

I clamp onto the flashlight as tight as I can and balance on my knees. She's standing face to face with me, which causes me to drop my flashlight again.

I'm in no hurry to stand up this time.

She's a little girl by the looks of her. Blond hair around her shoulders. White dress. The classic ghost I suppose. She's not looking at me. Well she is, but not exactly. She is looking through me. Like I'm not even there.

It takes everything I have to point the flashlight back in her face. Without the light, I can't see her. When she's in the light, there she is, in full Technicolor glory.

"Elise!" Abel yells, and there's a loud thud on the door. "Are you all right?"

Of course, I totally am. Not. "Yeah, just having a staring contest with the ghost."

Everything pauses. "Are you winning?"

"Yes, I forgot to tell you that one of my many skills is winning a staring contest with a thing that doesn't need to blink. Can you open the door, please?" I'm talking both to the ghost, who sort of reminds me of the ghost of Laura Ingalls Wilder, and Abel. Whoever can get me out of this room first will be my new best friend and hero.

I'm ready to get out now.

"I'm working on it!" Abel yells back. His voice sounds distorted somehow. Probably because it's an old house, the door is really thick, and my heart is roaring in my ears.

A bang at the door. Ghost girl doesn't move. Doesn't even flinch.

"Work faster." My legs are starting to shake. I don't know what this ghost is right off, but it isn't normal. That's pretty much a given, but there's something very off, something very confusing, and I think maybe if we figure out what, we can help it. She's not glitching like most ghosts. She's like sheer curtains, soft and flowy. I don't think I've ever seen anything like her.

That scares the crap out of me.

"I'm trying!" He hits the door again. Ghost girl never looks in his direction. She stares at me right in the eyes and keeps on mouthing what looks like the same thing she's been mouthing this entire time. I need to learn to read lips.

My hand is shaking as I slowly and gently, as to not irritate the thing I'm with, pull my phone out from my pocket. It takes a few swipes, but I finally hit the EVP app. It's worth a try.

Please don't let her jump at me.

Ghost girl smiles. She's looking through me to something right behind me .

Oh God, there's something behind me. I know there is. I can feel it on the back of my neck, but I can't turn around and look. My breathing comes in shallow spasms. I've got to hold it together. This isn't my first ghost encounter. I'm Elise Freakin' Morgan. I'm brave. I'm strong. I'm…

I feel a cool, soft breath on the back of my neck.

And all that mindset stuff about being strong, brave, and able just goes away. Whatever is behind me, can back the heck up.

"You came. I've been waiting for you." The EVP app is incredibly loud, and the words echo through the room.

Time to suck it up, princess, and go to work. It would be so much easier if this thing breathing on my damn neck would take a few steps back. Thanks so much. "I don't know who you think I am, but I'm not her. I promise."

"Elise!" Abel yells. He knocks on the door again. It doesn't budge. Just me in this dark room with my two new besties. Maybe Naked Girl can come over, and we can have a party, braid each other's rotting hair.

"You came. I waited for you," the EVP app says again.

Would she please stop saying that?

"Can you open the door?" Abel bangs, like that will do any good.

"I don't know." My voice is trembling. I'm afraid that if I move, either Laura Ingalls here, or whatever is breathing on my neck, will jump out at me, and that's not something I want to experience. "I can't move."

"Can't or won't?"

"Abel…"

"Are you scared? I didn't think you got scared."

Yes, Abel Hale, kick a girl while she's down. I appreciate that so much.

"How many ghosts are in there with you?" Finally, a helpful question.

"T-two." Laura Ingalls is the most still thing I've ever seen in my life. The fact that she's looking me right in the eyes, looking through me at whatever is behind me, isn't helping the matter at all. The hairs on my arms stand on end as my heartbeat rings in my ears.

She's going to get me.

"Who do you think they are?" Abel asks, as if he's helping. I wish he'd concentrate more on getting the door unlocked and less on this helpful banter.

"I don't think that's important right now. Please, open the door."

"Ask her." Abel is the conductor on the helpful train tonight.

"Ask her," I mumble. I'm a mumbler. "So… my name is Elise. What's yours?"

She just keeps right on staring through my eyes. "You came. I waited for you."

"What did she say?" Abel needs to beat the door down and get in here so he can hear her himself. I'm tired of being the in-between medium.

"She said for you to go screw yourself." I laugh. She doesn't.

"You came. I've been waiting for you." She smiles. I don't. What in the world…

Oh. My. Word.

I know exactly what we're dealing with here. "It's an echo," I shout to Abel. I anticipate his reply, so I mouth it with him. "What's an echo?"

"An echo," I keep going, "is a spirit stuck in a loop. Like a ghost imagine on a television if you don't change the channel fast enough and the image burns in."

"So, this girl isn't real?"

If only that were the case. "Oh she's very real, but I don't know if it a residual echo or a conscious echo."

He hits the door again. I wish he'd stop. It's only an echo. An echo can't hurt you. It's only living—or reliving—a moment in its life. A sad moment more than likely.

"Will it talk to you?" he asks.

I doubt it. Most echoes don't, except to say the same things over and over. I try anyway, just to make sure my theory is correct. "Can you hear me? My name is Elise." I fight to not say, "I'm here to help you" like I did on all our shows because I'm not there to help her. Truth is, I have no idea how to help her. She's stuck in this house forever, and there's nothing I can do to stop it.

This is where I feel powerless. I keep feeling like somewhere, deep down, even this echo has to know what's going on; she has to sense something, feel something. And to be trapped here, with whatever this thing is behind me, unable to be heard, must be maddening.

The door bursts open and in falls Abel.

My hero.

I have my flashlight shined on the girl, who hasn't moved. That's good. She can just stay right there.

It's unnerving, as much as all of this is unnerving, for her to be looking over me like this. I don't want to think there's something other than the echo in this house. Something more evil that's keeping her here. That would be incredibly sad. Especially since I can't save her.

I gave up trying to save the world a long time ago.

"Do you see her?" I ask when Abel is finally standing like a human.

"No," he says shortly, but I can see his expression change.

Something is up. He can feel something.

"She's right where my flashlight is. Are you sure you can't see her?"

"You came. I waited for you," my EVP app says. The girl smiles.

If these are the seconds before her death, all I have to say is ouch. That's low to be so excited to see someone and then die moments later. Die and become this horrible echo.

Abel looks around the room, squinting really hard. I think he's trying to see something. He's not going to do it that way. "What do you think it wants?"

I shrug. "Nothing, I don't think. I don't think it can feel."

"I think it can," he says, surprising me. "I think it can feel, and it's hurting right now."

"How... you can't know that."

Abel stands very straight. He quickly glances around the room, getting in his fight-or-flight stance. Something isn't right, other than everything that's going on here. "Something else is in here too."

I could have told him that. The freezing skin on the back of my neck is pretty good proof.

"What do you think it is?"

"No idea." He moves his flashlight around the room. "But it feels dark."

"It *feels* dark. How in the world do you know what anything feels like?"

I think it's a fine question. Abel, as is beginning to become our pattern, ignores my question. "We need to get out of here. Now."

His urgency is surprising. "Don't you want to get evidence of her?" I point to the echo that is still standing in relatively the same spot. She doesn't look scared or terrified. She looks, dare I say, peaceful. Unless you look in her eyes. They aren't wide or fearful, but there is something there, a twinkle, a darkness. I can't explain it, but it chills me. What if

Abel is right? What if this echo can feel? What if she's terrified?

"Elise, we have to go… now." He grabs my arm and tries to pull me out of the room. He's crazy if he thinks I'm going.

I jerk back. It's enough to keep him from getting me outside, but not enough to make him let me go. "I'm not going anywhere. You got me here. You wanted to go on a ghost hunt, well here we are. Hunting. Now that we see an echo, are you ready to leave?"

"It's not just an echo."

He's not wrong, but now I'm angry and set in my ways. "You don't know what you're talking about."

When I turn around, the echo is gone. "Great… just…" I push a few buttons so hard on my EVP app that the tip of my finger hurts. I mark the time and that the ghost disappeared. "Thanks for that."

I make sure to slam my shoulder into his arm as I leave the room. Him being made of rock, he didn't even flinch, and it might leave a bruise on my shoulder if I'm being honest, but I think I made my point.

Now, we'll have to hunt the echo back down again, maybe talk to her again, maybe not. Who knows if this is enough evidence for Julie? I mean, yeah, I got EVPs, but it's the same line over and over again. No video. No answers. It's going to take longer until I get home, longer until I can get my medicine and lie down… and let Naked Girl try to talk to me. If I close my eyes, I can ignore her… like a good friend would.

I stumble at the steps and grab onto the banister. My head is spinning. Stupid house. Stupid investigation. Stupid concussion. Stupid stress… all the freaking stress can go away! I'm done with it.

I'm done with everything.

I swat Abel's hand away. I don't want his comfort or his sympathy. I just want him to get me home.

Simple.

Easy.

Is that too much to ask?

"Leave me alone," I grumble when he doesn't let go.

"I'm not touching you."

I freeze.

His voice is from behind me... but not like right behind me. He's still close to the bedroom.

I'm leaning on the banister.

With something holding onto my arm.

"Elise?" Abel says very cautiously.

I don't want to look behind me... I don't wanna look behind me...

But I have to because I can't look like a chicken in front of Abel. I'm the professional ghost hunter after all.

And this won't be the first ghost I've ever seen.

Might be the first one that's ever touched me.

Might be the first one that's made my heart feel like it's going to explode out of my chest.

Might be the one that kills me.

Might be an easy way to die.

If I wait long enough, maybe it'll go away. Disappear so I won't ever have to see it.

If I wait...

It's not working.

The grip is getting tighter, and all I can think about is what happened to my mom. I can't let that happen to me.

I take a deep breath and slowly turn my head to the left.

My heart is beating in my ears. If this were a scary movie, the music would stop—preparing the audience for a jump-scare.

I don't like jump-scares.

The grip is tightening on my shoulder, so tight that I feel like it's cutting off my circulation.

My eyes meet hers.

She doesn't smile.

The echo. She sure as hell isn't echoing anymore.

I let out a shaky breath.

I squint at Abel, who is blinding me with the flashlight. "It's okay."

"Uh... you sure about that?"

Of course I'm sure about that. An echo wouldn't hurt anyone. I don't know why she's holding onto my shoulder, but it isn't trying to hurt me. If it were, I'd be down the steps by now. It isn't like she's not strong enough.

I back away, and she lets me. Her eyes, cold and hollow eyes, stare into mine. I wish I could help her. It's like going to the pound and seeing all the animals, knowing their fate, and not being able to help them all. That's how I feel seeing ghosts. I want to help them. I have no idea how.

"She's afraid," Abel says. Brave Abel Hale has not moved from his station at the bedroom door. Chicken.

"She probably was before she died. Echoes are souls who relive their last moments for eternity. It has to be a brutal hell."

"Were her last moments grabbing onto you?"

He sounds snarky. I'll try to control the urge to roll my eyes.

"No, but it could be, you know..." Okay, I know what it means. If it's an echo, it wouldn't be grabbing me because echoes just sort of echo. They aren't intelligent hauntings. This one, she's a hard one. I mean, she acts like an echo. She says the same thing, but she grabbed me.

Didn't she?

Oh God... oh, no.

"I don't think she touched me." The thought makes my breath hitch in my throat.

Abel nearly blinds me with the flashlight. "What?"

"I... don't think she touched me."

"Then what did?"

Well, how the hell should I know? "No idea. I didn't see anything but her."

I point to her. She's still looking at me. Her expression hasn't changed. Nothing about her has changed. Not even her position. But if she didn't touch me, then what did?

I feel like my head is going to explode. "Can we get out of here? My head can't take much more of this."

Either he didn't hear me, or he's totally ignoring me. "There is more than the echo here. I know it."

"Good for you." I step down to the first step. If he's all fired up about it, then he can investigate. Oh wait, he can't because he has no equipment, and he can't see ghosts.

Boo-hoo for him.

"Turn on your phone thingy," he says.

"My phone thingy?"

"The app thing you used before to hear her."

"Why? She'll say the same thing." Cause that's what echoes do.

"Humor me." I don't want to humor him. I want to get out of here. I hear his voice catch, though. He's desperate for any answer he can find, any clue to where his mother is. He's grasping at straws, but I was just like him. I can't keep this from him.

I nod and pull my phone from my pocket. I load the app and press record.

"You came. I've been waiting for you." The echo echoes from the landing on the stairs. Her tone is different now. More urgent. That's not like an echo. They never change. Never.

Never.

It's enough to get my attention. I steady myself on the banister and look up at Abel. Not my best idea. The world starts spinning, and I feel the world slipping out from under me. I'm never hunting ghosts with a concussion again.

"Hold on. I'm coming to help you." Abel makes it down one step before he screams and falls down on me. We both tumble down the stairs and don't stop until we hit hard at the bottom.

I land on top of him. My head is screaming, and my stomach is queasy. It's not just my concussion making me sick. It's the house, or whatever is in here.

The last time I felt this sick was with my mother.

I roll off Abel to let him breathe, but that's as far as I go. I'm down for the count. So stupid, to be done in by an echo. My dad would be proud. "You okay?" I ask.

"Fine." He groans and rolls on his belly. After waiting a second or two, he pushes himself up. Somewhere along the way, we lost the flashlight. I can't see him. I guess he can't see me.

And I can't see the ghost.

"That's not an echo," he says ever so helpfully.

"Ya think."

"It pushed me."

"It didn't push you. You lost your footing."

"Elise…"

"Abel."

Good, we know our names.

"Look, we need to get out of here."

No fighting from me on that.

"Take my hand," he says, and I almost break out laughing. Take his hand. I can't see his hand.

And I start to tell him that when the lights come back on—blinding me. I cover my eyes and roll over. My poor head will never forgive me.

"On a scale of one to ten, one being nothing and ten being Amityville… how bad would you rate this house?" He kneels beside me, rolls me over, and I think he's going to take my hand.

I'm wrong.

Instead, he scoops me up Rhett-Butler style and starts walking. Normally, I'd say something about it. I don't need anyone to carry me, except right now I do. I do believe this is the second time in two days I've needed him to help me.

I'm not excited about this.

What I am happy about is that I don't have to walk right now.

I'm happy that I can get out of the house without having to open my eyes because I don't think I can.

My stomach hurts worst of all. I don't know if it's from the concussion, the tumble down the stairs, or remembering the night my mother disappeared.

Or if it's from the evil in the house. The same evil in the house the night Mom died.

Either way, I'm afraid I'm going to throw up on him, and we can't have that.

I don't pray very often. I've never felt the urge to. I can't see how, if there's a Heaven, why some spirits have to stay here and some get to go. Maybe they've missed their door. I don't know. All I know is I don't pray a lot.

I'm praying right now.

I'm praying so hard that Abel gets me out of this house soon, and that I don't make a mess on either of us. That would be unprofessional.

I'm praying there isn't a dark spirit in here.

I'm praying I don't drop my phone.

I'm praying we get out of this house in one piece.

The door squeaks when he opens it. The porch creaks when he steps on it, and before I know it, he has me on the ground next to his car.

I lean against the cool metal and try my very best to open my eyes.

The door to the house slams shut.

Abel has never left my side.

"On a scale from zero to Amityville, huh?" I groan.

"Still think it's just an echo." Abel rubs my hair tenderly.

I think he's trying to make me feel better. It doesn't. The skin on my head feels super sensitive, and when he touches it, it's like thousands of pins stabbing me. I scoot away to get him to stop. It might have been nicer to use my words and just tell him to stop, but right now words aren't easy to find.

The only light around is coming from the house. Every single light is on.

Every single one.

I'm sure that's not how Julie left them.

"There's an echo in there. I know it." Course I have to concede that the echo isn't the only thing in there.

"Whatever's in there feels evil."

He sits down, not next to me, but close enough to catch me if I happen to fall over.

"How do you know what it feels like?" I've been dying to know. Between the hospital ghosts and these, how in the world does he know?

There's enough light coming from the house that I can see him. Not really well, but enough. He swallows hard. I wonder if he's going to tell me the truth or another lie. It isn't like I'm not keeping enough lies from him too.

"I can't see ghosts like you."

Good to know.

"But I can feel them."

"Say that again." The concussion must be affecting my hearing now.

"I can feel ghosts, their energy. I've been able to for as long as I remember. I felt that thing in my house."

"I saw your interview on TV before it went to hell, and you told my dad you didn't. You said you thought your mother was crazy." And his little sister too. I feel the heat firing up my cheeks. As someone who was repeatedly told she was crazy, I can't believe he'd do this!

"I know. I regret I ever said that."

"Then why did you?"

He hangs his head and picks up a stick. He taps it in his hand. "My dad. He was a drill sergeant. Not literally, but you know what I mean. I learned at an early age to not say much to him, not act weird or unusual. He hated that most of all. He was going to have a normal family, and by God, he was going to do anything he could to get it."

He clears his throat. "My sister didn't learn that lesson as well as I did. It wasn't her fault really. She was young, and she had my mom convinced. Truthfully, I think I felt it before she ever saw it."

"Saw what? What was that thing?"

He shakes his head. "I don't know. I never saw it, remember. Only felt it. It felt... it felt evil. Like pure evil. I can't describe it any other way than that."

"Screw your dad, weren't you afraid it would hurt you or your sister? Did you want to move?"

"Move where? We had everything, that's true. I've got my car; we had money. Outside we were happy. But the house, the voices, the... I don't know what my mom saw, but she looked terrified of it. I would hear her talking sometimes to no one. Talking to the air. Telling it to leave us alone, and that she was sorry."

"Sorry for what?"

"I don't know. She never told, and I never asked. Anyway, my mom had a nervous breakdown at work and lost her job. My dad had to pick up a second just to keep us above water. Outwardly, we were the Jones's everyone wanted to keep up with. Remember when I offered to pay your hospital bill?"

I nod.

"Well that was kind of a coping mechanism from my days at home. My parents never wanted anyone to know we didn't have money. I guess I'm the same way."

He hangs his head and continues. "Inside those walls, we were falling apart. There was no way he was going to move from a house that was already paid for just because his daughter had a wild imagination. The money was the only reason he agreed to be on *Dark and Deadly Things*. We needed it. He agreed to be on the show. More than that, I think he honestly thought he'd be vindicated. That there wouldn't be anything, and he'd be proven right. I don't know, maybe he wanted my sister to shut up about it."

The upstairs lights flicker in the Adams's house.

"But you knew." The longer I sit, the more he comes into focus. "You knew there was something there, and you did nothing."

In the case of my mother, I had no idea what was there was so powerful until it was too late.

Abel glares at me. "What could I do? Move? Take my sister and run away? There was nothing to do, so I was quiet about it."

"And you let it terrorize your little sister."

"I'd like to know how I was supposed to stop it."

I open my mouth and shut it with a sigh. "I'd like to know how to stop them too. I can see ghosts. I can see the pain on their faces, the hope fade when they realize I can't save them. I don't know what would become of them if I actually did. I see my mother, and I don't know what to do to bring her peace."

I still don't tell him I see his mother. There will be time for that later.

"I don't either. And I don't know how you do it. It's bad enough feeling them without seeing what they look like. To see them and not be able to help them..." He reaches for my hand, hesitates, and moves his hand back.

I'm sure that means something. I'm too sick to care.

"The echo in there isn't scary. She's sad. I mean, she looks horrible. Someone really messed her up when they killed her..."

"You think someone killed her?"

"Well, if they didn't, she sure had fun beating herself up."

He flinches and looks up toward the house. I don't see anything up there now, not in the window. Not in any window. I'm sure they're there, though, doing whatever ghosts do when they aren't scaring the heck out of people.

"What do we tell Julie? She can't go back in there."

"I'd say not." I should've asked about him before now. "How are you? Did you get hurt in the fall?"

He keeps his eyes on the house, but a hint of a smile pulls on his lips. "I'll live."

"You sure?"

He nods. "As sure as I can be. What I'm not sure of is what that other thing is in there."

"I didn't see anything else. Just the echo."

"Think it was the thing that killed the echo?"

I shrug. "I don't know. Could be anything, I guess. Maybe we should go home, let me rest and not die. I'm not as confident in myself as you are, and do more research in the morning. We can research the house, lore, legends, see what we might be dealing with."

"And if we figure it out? What do we do then?"

My heart sinks. "I have no idea."

CHAPTER EIGHTEEN

At around eleven o'clock, Julie comes home with Bethany sleeping in the backseat. It has to be way past her bedtime. I remember when I was six, my mom made me go to sleep around seven thirty. Entirely too early for ghost hunters, but my mom insisted on it. She wanted me to get plenty of sleep. She worried about things like that.

I take Julie away from the house to talk to her. Abel stays at the car and watches a sleeping Bethany.

All the lights in the house are still on. I'd hate to see her electric bill. Doubt the electric company will give her a discount for a haunting.

"You found it, didn't you?" Julie walks with me and hugs herself tightly.

It has gotten to be a bit chilly tonight, but not as cold as November usually gets around here. I think her chill is from knowing that something really bad is in her house. I would be cold too.

"We did." I can see why my dad and mom always said there was nothing inside. It would be easier.

"And?"

"And… and it's… I'm not sure what it is."

Her brow rises. "You aren't sure what it is."

"No, there's an echo. I know that for a fact. It's a girl, the one with the golden curls. It talked, so I could understand her on the EVP. Abel heard her."

"And you don't know what she is?"

There's a reason I never explained evidence to people. "I'm ninety percent sure she's an echo."

"And the other ten percent?"

Let's see if I can say this without totally freaking her out. "The other ten percent isn't sure. Something grabbed me by the shoulder. I don't know if it was the echo or not. By nature and definition actually, an echo is just like a glitch. They aren't conscious of what's going on around them. They are reliving their death over and over."

"Can they feel?"

Such an odd question. "I'm not sure. All I know is that this spirit had all the signs of an echo, except for one thing."

"What?"

I don't think she really wants to know.

"Her voice changed."

Julie backs up a bit. "Her voice changed?"

"She said the same thing over and over, 'You came. I knew you would.' But the inflection changed. That doesn't happen. It shouldn't happen. Think of an echo like a VHS tape. You remember those?"

She nods.

"Okay, every time you play a tape, the sounds, the words are exactly the same. There would be no reason for it to change. The echo in your house, changed, ever so slightly. It was enough to make me notice. Imagine Jack from *Titanic*. What if his inflection changed when he told Rose to never let go? You'd pick up on it if you'd watched the movie enough."

And I had.

"So what does that mean for me? Is the echo, or whatever

it is, dangerous?"

The question we get asked more than anything else. "Truthfully, I'm not sure. And I'm not sure it's the only ghost in your house."

She waits.

I keep going. "There's something else. Something I can't place. It's dark, though. Evil."

She raises her fingers to her lips. Maybe I should've been more tactful than that.

"I mean... okay, I don't want to scare you." Famous last words. "But it pushed Abel down the stairs. Took me down with him. And see all those lights? They weren't on when we left. Actually, they all went off when it became dark, and we had to use flashlights. Then when we got out of the house, it lit up like a Christmas tree."

Julie hugs herself tighter as she turns toward her house. I wonder what's going through her mind. None of it can be good. This was supposed to be her place to start over, not turn into a horror movie.

She lost her husband at such an early age. That's enough horror to go around.

"Do you think... do you think it might be my husband? Do you think he could have followed us here?"

I hadn't thought about that. "Was your husband violent? Or do you think he would be if he felt his family was threatened?"

Julie doesn't answer. She starts walking toward the house slowly. By the tilt of her head, I can tell her gaze is fixed on the windows.

"Julie." I run and catch up with her. My head wishes I hadn't. I need some pain pills and a bed, quick. I grab her arm and turn her toward me. She's pale. Very pale. "Look, you can't stay here tonight. Take Bethany and go somewhere else."

"I don't have anywhere else to go."

"Find a hotel or something, okay? It'll be worth it, trust

me. Go to a hotel, rest, relax. Tomorrow, Abel and I will do some research on the house. We'll see what could be inside and come up with some ways to maybe get rid of it."

"Maybe?"

"We've never gotten rid of one before. Not even on my dad's show."

Julie takes a deep breath and looks from the house to the car. Abel is sitting in the driver's seat. The car is humming, and soft music is playing through the air.

Abel rolls the window down. "I didn't want her to get cold."

Julie smiles. "Thank you for taking care of her. Thank you both." She takes my hands and squeezes them. "I know it was out of your way to come here, you being hurt and all, but I appreciate it so much."

I squeeze her hands back. "Please, please, don't go back into that house until Abel and I have a chance to figure out what's inside. There may be a way we can help you."

I hope we can help her.

I need to help her.

For my own sanity.

Why have this gift and not be able to use it for good or to help people?

"Thank you, for everything." She squeezes my hand again before letting it go.

Abel gets out of the driver's seat, and Julie slides in.

"We'll see you later." Abel waves. "I'll call you as soon as we find something."

Julie nods as she rolls up the window. She drives away with a small wave and a faraway look in her eye.

"Let's get you home," Abel says.

I'm not opposed to that. "What about all those lights?"

He turns and stares at the house too. "I don't want to go back in there."

"Me either. It'll be there tomorrow." I'm in desperate

need of my painkillers and sleep. Tomorrow will be a long day.

CHAPTER NINETEEN

MY FATHER HAD ALWAYS BEEN THE businessman of the operation. He knew how to sell *Dark and Deadly Things* to a network that wasn't really even looking for a ghost show. He was good at his job, good at selling and at making people buy what he was selling.

My mother was the heart of the show. She was the one that comforted terrified mothers who were so scared that their child would be hurt by the thing inside their house. And no matter what we found—or what we saw—we always told the parents there was nothing to be worried about. We'd have EVPs of ghosts saying they wanted the people out. I'd see ghosts physically getting ready to attack, but we never mentioned any of that to the client. At all.

That would be bad for business.

Silas and I were the love story. We were the network's hope to revive the series after the scandal of season eight. And it worked for a time. Newer viewers came on. Silas looked good in night vision. Everything was fine in the world again.

Until it wasn't.

Silas changed overnight after my mom died. One day he

was the sweetest guy, and the next he was a bastard. No matter what the network said, I couldn't stay with him. I couldn't. So I did what anyone else would do, I dumped him, and the ratings suffered.

When production started up again, Silas was promoted to lead investigator, and I quit the show.

My dad loved me...

My dad loves me.

But it's always been and will always be business.

Silas gave us high ratings. It wasn't personal, but I couldn't help taking it that way. Especially since he took Mom's spot.

Jerk.

My head will not stay up anymore. My head's on the nice cool window as Abel drives me back to my dorm. I don't care if the photographers are there. I don't care if the Pope is there, truth be told. I don't even care if there are fifteen ghosts in my room all screaming my name.

I'm going to bed.

I'm pulling the covers over my eyes.

And I'm not getting up until tomorrow when I have to go dig through the history of the Adams house. They can't make me.

I just hope he doesn't want to leave early. It's after midnight, and my land, I'd love to sleep.

Sleep... ahhhh...

"I understand now why my father never wanted to give homeowners bad news." I didn't mean to say it out loud. Now that I have, well, I guess we'll talk about it.

Abel, who's been humming away to Kansas, stops humming. "He told my mom there was nothing to worry about."

Well, of course he did. Now I really wish I hadn't brought it up.

"I'm sorry. I really am. About everything. What

happened to your family. About being stuck here with me when I'm sure you'd rather be anywhere else."

I hug the bag of prescription medicine tighter to my chest like a security blanket. I'm spent, so tired, and I'm sure that whatever he says to me, I'll probably start crying. I don't want to cry, so I hold on for dear life.

"What happened to my family wasn't your fault."

Then why does it feel like it is?

"I don't even know if it's your father's fault, though he's the easy one to blame."

"Why does everyone blame him and not Silas?" All this no-filter stuff and saying whatever's on my mind is going to get me in trouble. Oh sweet bed, take me away.

"Do you think Silas would intentionally throw himself across the room and give himself all those bruises?"

"No."

"Then maybe your father is the easiest to blame because he was the least injured?"

Because my filter is gone, I say what I've wanted to ask for two days. "Do you think my father did it?"

Abel doesn't answer right away. He keeps his hands calmly on the steering wheel and his eyes on the road. "I don't know what I believe. I know my dad and little sister are dead. I have no idea where my mom is or if she's even alive."

My stomach knots.

"But I don't think it was your father. I felt something. Something was in that room with us. The same thing I'd felt in the house since we moved in."

"The same thing you felt in Julie's house?"

He shakes his head. "No, not exactly. Similar, but I can't explain it. Whatever was or still is in my house, it was pure evil."

"You said the thing in Julie's house was evil."

"I know. Like I said, I can't explain it. It just felt different. I don't know if it was the same type of spirit or not. Or if the thing in my house felt stronger because it was my house. All I know is that I never want to feel something like that again. Have you ever seen something like that?"

I don't want to answer. I want to sleep. My mouth runs away again. "Once. It was on a hunt six months ago."

"The night your mom disappeared?"

He didn't have to bring that up. It isn't like my mother's death is a secret. My family was on television. That comes with a certain level of notoriety. Good and bad. My mom's death, or her disappearance as it was deemed, was even in *TV Guide*.

Still, I don't like to talk about it. I don't want to think about it, and if I'm not careful with as much gunk that is going around in my head right now, I am afraid I'll blurt out about his mother.

I should tell him.

Lord knows I should.

And I will...

Tomorrow.

Before we go to the library and look up everything we can find on the Adams house. I'll bear my soul and tell him all about his mother. I won't leave him in the dark any longer than he needs to be.

I just can't tonight.

I'm being selfish. I know it.

I'm just afraid he won't want anything else to do with me when he finds out about his mother. It might be silly. I'm not exactly thinking clearly at the moment. If I'm wrong, I'm sure I'll pay for it. He might hate me forever.

At least I have tonight.

Abel places his hand over mine. I feel at peace.

Happy even.

Content.

Calm.

Peaceful.

"You've had a long day," he says the obvious.

I mumble, "Uh-huh." I'll be asleep soon. I might not even make it back to my room. It's warm in his car. The bloodstains have been cleaned. It's nice in here. Nice and calming, and I can close my eyes and sleep.

"Elise," he whispers, rubbing his thumb in circles over my hand.

I'll be asleep in no time.

"Hmm…"

"Can ghosts travel from place to place? Follow someone maybe?"

That's way too much talking for me tonight. "Um… hum…" It's the last thing I remember.

Everything is black.

I don't dream.

Thank the Lord, I don't dream.

CHAPTER TWENTY

I HAVE NO IDEA HOW I got in my bed.

I don't even know how I got my pajamas on.

I think Naked Girl knows.

She's smiling at me from across the room. She's biting on her lip, and dare I say, she's about to jump out of her skin... not literally of course. She doesn't have skin.

Naked Girl knows something I don't know...

And she's dying to tell me.

Ha-ha... so many jokes this morning.

"You look happy today." It's pretty distressing to see Naked Girl so happy. She's, for lack of a better visual, a bloody mess. Her face is all carved up. She has a big slash on her neck, and I've never counted her stab wounds, but I imagine there are over eleven.

So, to see her smile... it's a bit weird.

She nods. Yup. She's happy.

"Did Abel bring me in last night?"

She nods again.

Maybe I should do this with my mom. Play five thousand questions until I figure out what happened to her. Shouldn't take long…

"Did Abel change my clothes and put me to bed?"

Her brows furrow, and she stands, all offended, and points to her chest.

"You did it?"

She nods.

Well, that's a new development. "You… you took my clothes off and put new ones on me?"

There's that smile again.

"But… you're a ghost. How can you move things?" That seems entirely impossible.

At least everything I know about ghosts says that ghosts may be able to move things, but they sure can't strip a girl down to her drawers and put her pjs on. That one's not in the lore.

Yet.

I think I've hurt her feelings. She rolls her eyes and marches for the door. Like she needs to open it to go out. "Wait, wait… I'm sorry, okay. I'm just not used to this. Most ghosts can't communicate with me. Much less, you know, tuck me in."

Naked Girl turns toward me. Again her eyes narrow, and she mouths something I can't figure out.

My head isn't hurting as bad this morning. If my day keeps going in this direction, my head will hurt soon enough.

"I don't understand," I admit, begrudgingly.

She can't seem to hide the smirk.

"Oh! I get it. You're messing with me. I hate to tell you, but my brain has been scrambled enough the last few days." It really has. "Did you see who changed my clothes? Was it Abel?"

Naked Girl nods and starts moving her lips like she's telling me something vitally important. I can't hear her.

Wait…

I hold up my hand to stop her and grab my bag, looking

for my phone so I can pull up the EVP app.

While I'm searching, my door opens—did I not lock it?—and in walks Abel Hale. He doesn't stop to greet me, smile, hug, or shake my hand. Nothing.

He comes in, out of breath. "We have to go."

"Where?" I jump up and don't even try to regain my modesty. It isn't like I'm wearing a Victoria's Secret skimpy gown. Even if I were, I know Abel couldn't care less. He put me in the dang clothes after all.

"Julie Adams's house."

That certainly grabs my attention. I grab the closest pile of clothes I can find and start putting them on. Abel, much to my chagrin, turns his back to me. Chalk it up to him being gentlemanly. "What's wrong with her house. Did something happen last night?"

"We have to go. Now. Meet me outside in no more than five minutes." With that, he walks out the door, leaving me incredibly perplexed, and Naked Girl incredibly irritated."I bet he found something," I tell Naked Girl, who looks like she's about to cry. "No… don't do that. I promise when I get back, we will try the EVP thing and see if I can hear you, okay?

I don't even get all the words out. One minute I'm talking. The next, Naked Girl is nowhere to be seen. I finish getting ready; put my phone in my pocke; grab my coat, my bag, and my pain pills; and lock the door behind me.

When I get inside Abel's car, he's sitting in the driver's seat. He throws his phone in his lap and grips the steering wheel. This isn't someone who's singing his favorite song. This is a man who's mad at the world.

What in the world could've happened from when he dropped me off at whatever o'clock last night and now? I'm almost too scared to find out.

CHAPTER TWENTY-ONE

"Took you long enough." He bitches when I get in and shut the door. Normally calm boy isn't calm.

I'll make a note of that.

"Had to brush my teeth. Nothing like clean breath." I'm trying to make light of the situation. He seems so far from it.

"Okay, what's wrong?"

He bites his lip. For the first time, I notice that his eyes are red and so are his cheeks. He's either sad or pissed off. Maybe both. Usually he's the calm one. The one who makes me feel better when he shouldn't. I can't make him calm. I've never been good at making anyone calm or feel better.

Abel needs to get out of this funk now.

Again, I'm being selfish.

My stomach knots tighter. I want my pain pills, but I don't want to take them if we're going to Julie's. Ghost hunters shouldn't be high on pain pills. Rule of thumb. I was reminded of that last night.

What if... just what if... he found out about his mother? What if something happened while he was gone, or what if I admitted something while I was conked out? What if I told him about his mother, and now he's ticked?

He'd have every right to be ticked.

I'd be ticked.

That has to be what it is.

I should tell him I'm sorry. At least get him talking to me again. I start to say those very words when he cuts me off. "Julie Adams. We need to get to her house as fast as we can."

I just... "What? Why?"

"A feeling."

"A feeling? You got me out of the house this morning for a feeling. I thought someone had died as much as you've moped."

"Someone might if we don't stop it."

"Stop what?"

"Stop whatever is in that house."

I rub my fingers over my temples. "We've gone over this. We have no idea how to stop it. That's the problem. The best thing for her to do is to high tail it and get the heck out of dodge."

"I don't think that'll work."

"Why?"

"Because... I think the dark ghost, the evil one, is her husband."

"At the house?"

"Yes."

"At her house? The house she's currently occupying?"

"Yes, Elise. Why is that so hard to comprehend?"

Well, one because of the concussion and two... "Because ghosts normally stay in one location, mainly where they die. Like the echo. She's where she died. She's there. She died there."

"Did she?" He has a tone. I don't like his tone.

"Yes." I sound very sure of myself.

"Okay, fine. Say the echo has been there since she died and isn't really a threat. So that leaves the evil thing. What if it's new, and that's why the echo is stirred up? What if it followed the Adams family here? What if it's her husband? She said it herself; he wasn't very nice. What if there's more to the story than she's letting on? What if it isn't the house at all, not really? What if it's whatever they brought with them?"

Good Lord, that's a lot of what-ifs.

I don't remember it like that. Sure she seemed to get a different look about her when I mentioned the ghost, and then she got quiet when I mentioned her husband.

I was too busy daydreaming about my bed and my covers. I was selfish.

I didn't take the time to make sure my client was okay.

Ghost hunting rule number two.

"Do you think she's at the house right now?"

"I know she is."

"How do you…?"

"I just know, okay? She's there, and it's going to get really bad if we don't help her."

He's speeding, and I grab onto the grip above my door to steady me. "Say her husband did come with her, say he's in the house with her, say he's violent, what in the world are we supposed to do to keep her safe? There's no way we can get rid of him."

"We'll have to think of something."

That's very reassuring. Let's speed toward the angry ghost dude without a plan. There's no way this will backfire on us.

"Why would she go back to that house? We told her to stay away."

He speeds up, and I clamp on tighter. At this rate, we will need the siren from Ecto-1. "Maybe to make sure it was her husband. Maybe her daughter forgot something. How should I know? The point is: she went back."

"And you know this how?" I ask again.

Secrets and lies.

"Doesn't matter. Now we need to brainstorm ways to get rid of him before he hurts her again."

"You don't think ghost hunters have been trying to find the answer to that for years? No one knows. Not really."

Abel taps on the steering wheel. "You have seventeen minutes to come up with something. Do it fast."

CHAPTER TWENTY-TWO

ABEL'S BACK TIRES SLIDE AS HE pulls into the gravel driveway at Julie Adams's house. The sun is barely up, and all the lights in the house are still on, just like we left them.

Julie's car is parked in front of the door.

"How did you know?"

"Answers, Elise. We need answers to how we're going to save her and her daughter. Focus on that."

Focus on that. I can barely focus on breathing. Of all the times to have a concussion.

Okay, focus… focus…

If this is the ghost of her dead husband, then he has to have followed her. That means he's attached to something. If he's attached to something, all we have to do is find out what that something is, and either send it away or bury it. Heck, we can even burn it and see if that works.

The problem would be finding the thing he's attached to, and then hoping getting rid of it actually works.

I don't know if it'll work.

It's the only theory I can come up with that doesn't involve proton packs.

Abel slams on the breaks and jumps out of the car. I go with him, only not as fast. "Please tell me you have something," he yells as he climbs the third step.

"I have a theory." And it's only that. A theory. I've never done it, and I've never seen it proven.

"That's a start." He reaches the top step and runs for the door. He has his hand up to knock when he stops and points. "It's open a little."

The lights flicker.

"Shit," he says, kicking the door open. He runs inside. I'm too late. It slams in my face and locks.

"Abel!" I scream and pound on the door. "Abel! Open the door!"

"I'm trying!" The handle jiggles in my hand. He pulls it open a crack, far enough for me to see him. His eyes widen, and then he's pulled from my view. The door slams shut.

"Abel!" I scream, pushing on the door with everything I have. It's no use.

I hear laughing from inside the house.

It's coming from a little girl.

CHAPTER TWENTY-THREE

I'M TRAPPED OUTSIDE.

Abel is trapped inside.

I run around the porch, looking for anything I can use to beat the door down with. I'm not strong, not really, and with a paranormal entity inside, there's no way I can get that door open. I know that.

I also know there are two big windows, floor to ceiling windows, on the outside of the house.

I can break those.

I find a planter with flowers that probably bloomed three years ago next to the door and, without thinking it through, slam it into the window. Shattered pieces scatter into the house.

I jump in and instantly wish I had a plan.

The furniture is on the ceiling. Perfectly placed on the ceiling like a dollhouse that's been turned upside down.

A small table, a child-sized table, is on the floor in the middle of the foyer. It has a white sheet spread across it and two child-sized chairs sitting around it. Bethany is sitting there. Along with the echo. Bethany is smiling.

The echo, who resembles Bethany, looks terrified.

"You came," she mouths. I can't hear her, but I can tell what she's saying since it is the only thing she does say. Her eyes scream for help. "I knew you would."

I... am not ready for this mess. I retreat toward the window, only to find it already fixed. All the broken glass is gone. The window is fully intact. There's no way out.

"You came into my home." Bethany looks me dead in the eyes. Her voice isn't hers. It's a man's. "You tried to hurt my family. I won't let anyone hurt my family." She pours tea for her and the echo. "No one."

I don't know whether to move forward or back. I look around to see if I can find Abel or Julie. Abel is hanging to the banister by his hands. He looks at me, his eyes wide. If he's asking if I've ever seen anything like this before, the answer is no. I don't know what to do.

"Where's your mother?" I try talking to the little girl. Maybe, she can answer me, and maybe she can push the male spirit out of the way.

Bethany glares at me and tilts her head. A chair falls from the ceiling, swoops me up, and slides me over to the table. She calmly places a teacup in front of me and pours some of the pretend tea. The echo starts to shake.

"My mother died in 1999. I was eight years old. The doctor said it was a suicide. It wasn't."

"Did someone k-kill your mother?"

Bethany places pretend sugar into my teacup. "I did," the male voice says.

"Why?" I'm shaking like the echo.

Bethany shrugs. "She wouldn't let me go to my neighbor's house. We were best friends. We did everything together. I'd go there after school. I'd stay until late at night. And my friend, her name was Amanda, she liked having me over. She loved me. She told me once she loved me, and I believed her." The male voice boomed through Bethany's tiny lips. "I believed her, and my mother took her away from me. She said Amanda told her family lies about me. Said I'd touched her, made her do things… I was eight years old."

Eight years old.

"Everything I did to her was things she liked, things she wanted. She wanted me to hold her down. She wanted me to feel up her skirt. I knew she did. She said she loved me."

The echo shivers. I don't think she's an echo anymore. "You came. I knew you would."

Bethany glances at me. "She says that all the time. Can't she say anything else?"

"No. I don't think so."

"Pity. She's a pretty thing."

Yes, she is. A pretty thing whose life was probably cut short so quickly that she didn't realize she was dead for the longest time. I think this encounter has woken her up in a way.

"Who are you?" I ask to make small talk. I know who he is.

Bethany sneers as she adds sugar to her pretend tea. "Do you know that Bethany's mother, my wife, actually tried to leave me? She said I wasn't the man she thought I was. She said she wanted me out of her daughter's life. She said she never wanted me to see her again. Is that how any wife should treat her husband? Should any mother keep a child's father away from her?"

In this case, probably.

"No," I answer because I want to live.

"No. And she did. She told Bethany all kinds of things. I can hear them, screeching around in her mind. She told her I was evil. That I didn't love her. Bethany knew that wasn't true. She wanted to live with me."

"So you made that happen." It isn't a question.

Bethany smiles. "I made that happen."

She looks up just as a body starts descending from the ceiling. Julie. It isn't until she's almost to me that I see her eyes

165

blink. She's not dead, not yet, but by the looks of it, it could happen at any minute.

Her hands are tied over her head like Abel's, only unlike Abel, Julie has been sliced by what looks like claws. My gaze automatically goes to Bethany's hands. Sure enough, there's blood on her fingernails.

Julie's eyes roll back in her head. Bethany stops before her feet touch the floor, only her tiptoes scrape the hardwood. "She killed me, you know? Shot me in the head. Right..." He points to Bethany's temple. "Here. I wasn't expecting it. Imagine sitting down to a nice dinner and then BAM!" A high-pitched shot screams through the room, and I duck. Bethany laughs. "Exactly. I saw a light, and I'd be damned if I'd go toward it. This is my life. My family. And there ain't nothing, not even death, going to take me away from it. So, I refused to go. And I hitched a ride on Julie's wedding ring."

Her wedding ring? Seems kind of risky. "It was her grandmother's, so I knew she wouldn't leave it. And I knew she wouldn't wear it to work and be reminded of me. She's a bitch that way. So, it felt like a safe bet. Sure enough, she couldn't stand to live in the house. I made sure to make it a living hell for her."

Julie hadn't mentioned anything about paranormal activity in their old house. She said it started when she got here. She lied. Lied to cover up the fact that she killed her husband? From what I can tell, he deserved it.

"Bethany... Mommy's here." Julie coughs and blood comes out. "Mommy's here. I won't let him hurt you, but you have to fight him. You fight him. You fight him like you did that night in your room."

Abel's eyes catch me.

No.

No...

"You fight him, baby, and I'll take care of him." The rope pulls her up before she gets her sentence out. I hear bones cracking a few seconds later. I hope to God it wasn't her neck.

Bethany screams.

Not the male voice, not her father, but Bethany. "Bethany." I lean over and take her hands. She's cold and clammy. "Bethany, remember me? I'm Elise. I'm a friend of your mother's. I'm here to help you. Okay, you have to let me let help you, and you've got to fight your father. Can you do that for me?"

She nods.

Her father laughs.

"She doesn't want your help." His voice is back, coming from Bethany's lips. "She doesn't want anyone's help. She doesn't need it. How I show my love to my child is my business, do you understand?"

"You're sick." The words seep out before I can stop them. It might not be the best idea to taunt the incredibly disturbed poltergeist, but damn it, this is insane. "You're sick, and you've got to stop hurting your daughter."

"I'd never hurt her."

A tear falls down Bethany's cheek. My Lord, she's awake in there.

"I never hurt her before. I won't hurt her now. I want to be together. I want us to be a family, and her bitch of a mother took that away from us. Self defense my ass!" The table flies across the room, smashing inches from Abel. Shards of glass cut his face and arms, sending little red rivers down his skin.

"You're a bastard!" I stand and scream at the monster inside the little girl. "You're an evil, vile thing, and I won't let you take control over that girl anymore!"

Wind picks up in the room, blowing my hair all around my head. Paper, trinkets, anything and everything starts to fly clockwise.

Bethany glares at me. "You have no choice. You're just a woman. Just like her mother. And there's nothing in this life or the next that'll get me away from my daughter. Nothing. She's mine. I'm with her always, and you can go to hell." She moves her hand and flings me across the room.

My back slams against the door, knocking the wind out of me. I can't move. Can barely breathe.

The echo closes her eyes. "You came. I knew you would," she mouths.

I wonder if this is the same way she died.

"Craig!" Julie screams from the ceiling. I can see her feet dangling. "Don't you dare hurt our little girl."

"Oh!" She stands and dances a little jig. She has on a white gown, and her hair is falling loose around her shoulders. "So, it's our little girl again. Our. Do you remember what you said to me that night? You said she'd never be mine. You said we were finished, and there was no way I'd ever see you or her ever again. Do you remember that? Because I sure as hell do! I wasn't meaning to do this, but then you brought in ghost hunters. I remember that one from television." She motions in my direction. "And I knew... I knew my time was limited. She'd try to get rid of me, and she'd succeed."

He has more faith in me than I do.

"I couldn't let that happen. Don't you see? We're a family again." He lowers Julie down from the ceiling. He stops her when she gets close enough to the floor for her feet to touch, and he lets her arms go. She falls to her knees on the floor and doubles over. "I can't take care of Bethany myself. I'm not stupid. I know CPS will come knocking, just like they did at home when she went and blabbed to her stupid teacher.

"So... I'll let you live. You can go on with your life. You can be a part of Bethany's. That's much more than you offered me. However, if you try anything, if you tell anyone... they'll think you are crazy. If they happen to believe you, I'll rip out Bethany's heart the same way you ripped out mine. I don't care if she's my daughter. She is also yours."

Another tear slides down Bethany's cheek.

"Do you understand me, Julie?"

Julie looks at me, helpless. It's exactly how I feel.

It's then that I see the ring on her finger. Her ring finger on her married hand. Her ring... the ring. "Fireplace." I mouth the word and motion toward her hand.

She doesn't seem to click. "Fireplace." I fight the invisible elephant sitting on my chest. "Fireplace! Fireplace! Throw it in the fireplace!"

No sooner do the words come out of my mouth than Julie rips the wedding ring from her finger and throws it as hard as she can into the fire.

Bethany roars. She runs to the hearth and digs through the ashes. Bethany's screams mix with her father's.

"Stop!" I yell, trying to free myself from the door. He's going to hurt her. He's going to kill her if he doesn't stop.

Abel closes his eyes, and a wave of calm takes me over. It doesn't last long, and it doesn't stop Craig, but it does make him hesitate long enough for me to get free. I run toward them, ready to pull Bethany from the fire.

The echo beats me to it. She throws herself into the fire—screaming, scorching—and pushes Bethany out. Bethany falls backwards. Her father's spirit stays where it is. The echo has him by the arm.

I see his mouth move. He's screaming no. The echo looks at me and smiles. She doesn't scream as the fire takes her over. Craig fights and screams, everything he can to get away from her. He goes up in a blaze of smoke too.

It stops.

Everything on the ceiling and floating around the room falls to the floor. Julie runs over and flings herself on top of her daughter to shield her from the falling debris.

Abel runs over to me and pulls me into his arms. I let him hold me.

CHAPTER TWENTY-FOUR

THE POLICE CAME.

The ambulance came.

They took Bethany and Julie to the hospital. Since none of us really knew what to tell the cops or the doctors, we all agreed to say it was a burglar. Bethany remembers, though. That's the part I hate the most. I hope she can handle it. She's only eight. But I guess she doesn't have a choice.

Things happen, and we have to somehow find the strength to get through it and live our lives.

I stand next to Abel as the ambulance drives away. He reaches for my hand, and I take it. The morning sun is rising. There isn't a cloud in the sky. It's a new day. I wonder if he feels it like I do.

****

"SO, DO YOU WANT to stop for breakfast?" He sounds tired, maybe even a little nervous. After this morning, I don't think he has anything to be nervous about.

Breakfast doesn't sound good. I'm not in the least bit

hungry. I keep seeing Bethany in my mind. Scared. Terrified. Having her father's spirit inside her, the father that did God knows what to her. How do you deal with that? I know you move on, and that's all she can do, but still... how do you do it?

"Maybe another time." I hope he asks me again. I hope this isn't the last time I see him. I wouldn't doubt if it is. "I guess this means you want to go investigate your house now. I lost the bet."

He actually laughs. "I'm not sure about right now. I think I need some time to process what happened at the Adams house."

I feel the same way.

"Have you ever in your years of ghost hunting had a case end like that?"

"You mean end with an eight-year-old girl possessed by the ghost of her abusive father that her mother killed and made it look like a suicide?"

"Yes." He sighs. "That."

I lean my head back against the seat and wince. My head still hurts. Being thrown around like a ragdoll didn't help anything. Stupid ghosts. "Can't say that I have. Truthfully, I never thought much about the cases after we left, and even less after we started filming it for television. Then it was just, I don't know, easier to pretend they were actors, or people egging it on to get on television for one reason or another. This... this was a whole new level of real."

"Then I'm glad I got to be a part of it." He rubs his fingers over his chin. I think he's about to ask me something I don't want to answer.

"How many people do you think have a ghost or, hell, even a paranormal problem?"

A paranormal problem... that's one way to put it. "I don't know. More than I ever thought possible, truth be told. I can't imagine things out there like this. And that echo..."

"She saved us all."

I have to agree. "It's like she snapped out of her loop and went on. It's like…"

"It's like we saved her." Abel stops at the red light and looks in my direction.

"I think she saved herself."

"We helped."

"You were attached to the banister, and I was thrown against the wall. I don't know how much we helped."

"You knew to throw the ring in the fire," he reminds me as the light turns green.

"It was a guess. It was all I could think of doing at the moment. I didn't what him to hurt Bethany."

I'm sure when I call and check on her later, they'll say she has second- and third-degree burns on her arms. I think she'll be okay though. Physically. I hope she is. I might even pray about it. Not that I'll tell anybody. No sense in getting anyone else worked up.

"There are a lot of people who need help." Abel catches me off guard with that sort of vague statement. Yeah, I suppose there are.

"Yeah, some were on television to be on television. We even had this family once try to fake evidence so we'd say their house was haunted and they could list it for more."

"Does that actually work?"

"They seem to think so. I know my dad figured out every trick they had, and I found zero ghosts, so they were thoroughly debunked. It was a humiliating episode. I think it's only aired once."

He drums his fingers on the steering wheel. "Sounds like someone tried to pull the wool over your dad's eyes. I can't imagine anyone ever doing that."

I had to laugh. So many people had tried. So many had failed. "And they all thought they were cleaver too. This one guy actually rigged up a bed so the sheets would move. And this one person put a picture in the mirror of the bathroom so it would light up like a ghost was behind you when you went in. It was insane."

"People will do all sorts of things to get on television."

"You're telling me. I think it's crazy myself. I never really liked it."

"Being on TV?"

I nod. "It was too demanding. Too much pressure. I just liked investigating. I miss how it used to be with my dad and mom. We'd go to a house to investigate, and I really felt like we were helping people. Course that was before the ghost dry spell and the evidence faking."

I don't say anything for a minute. My dad and Bethany's dad were not the same, but they had so much in common. My dad didn't ever do anything bad to me, so there's that, but he was controlling sometimes.

"Are you thinking about your dad and Bethany's dad?"

The man tends to always know what I'm feeling. I'm not sure how I feel about that. "Yeah. I can't help it. It sort of fits."

"I didn't know your dad much, and yeah, I went off on him in the hospital. But, I don't for a second think he's anything like Bethany's dad. That man was insane."

"My dad *is* in an insane asylum," I remind Abel.

"Not the same thing. Being in one and needing to be in one are two different things. I want you to know that I don't think your father is like Craig Adams. I don't. I don't want you to think he is either."

"My dad..." Why am I telling him this? "My dad always said that it took a miracle for me to be born."

"Miracle?"

"Yeah, see all the doctors told my mom she couldn't have kids. Like ever. She had something going on with her. I don't know exactly. But lo and behold, they got me. I've seen my mom's pregnant belly pictures, so I know I'm not adopted, and they told me I wasn't. It was a miracle. And now look how it ended."

It's so sad to think a couple who tried so hard to have a baby, who gave everything they had, finally got what they prayed for. And that ended up being me... a freak who sees ghosts. I bet I wasn't what they asked the stork for.

"Life has a funny way about it," Abel says absently.

"It does." I spend time thinking about my parents. In their photos before I was born—when my mom was pregnant with me—they looked so happy. Like they had the entire world to look forward to. I don't remember them looking that happy after I was born, at least from what I recall. My mom loved me. My dad loved me. But I'm not sure they still loved each other. I hate that. I wish they had at least lived happily ever after.

I wonder how Abel's dad is. I haven't seen him. And I haven't seen Abel's sister either since she died. Only his mom. I want to know why. Or maybe I don't. Maybe some questions and some ponderments are better left unknown. Leaves a little mystery in life.

"I wonder... I wonder if you can do anything like that and save your mother." He glances in my direction.

"My mother isn't stuck in a loop. My mother... I don't know what she is actually."

I finally glance at my phone and see that Silas has messaged me fifteen times. Silas... I was supposed to meet him at my mom's house tonight! "Ugh," I groan and throw my head back against the seat.

"What is it now?"

"Silas. I forgot. I was supposed to meet him. He has some evidence he wants to show me from your house."

That certainly catches his attention. "My house? As in he thinks he caught the thing that killed my family on camera, and you didn't happen to mention it. Didn't think that maybe I'd like to go and look at it."

"I wanted to see what it was before I got your hopes up."

He scoffs and puts the car in drive. He pulls away, and I have to scramble to pull the door closed. "If we've learned anything from this, it's that you have to stop trying to protect my hopes. I can take care of them myself, thank you very much. As for Silas, since it's my house, I say I get to see the evidence he found too. Don't you?"

Do I have a choice? "You sure you're up for it? I mean, it got really hairy at Julie's house? You said you weren't ready to go back to your house. Do you think you can watch a video about it?"

He doesn't look at me. "I don't have a choice."

CHAPTER TWENTY-FIVE

I DON'T TELL SILAS I'M BRINGING Abel to this little video-watching shindig. I figure he'll find out when we got there... and we got there.

It isn't my mother's house actually. It's my grandmother's that my mom inherited when my grandma died. Thank the Lord my grandma went on over to the other side and isn't still sticking around. It would be sad if she did. My grandmother wasn't a very kind soul. Well, she was sometimes, I suppose. But she always had something negative to say. She died when I was eight, and I still remember how she used to tell me to stand up straight and stop acting like a boy. She was very big on that. I was supposed to be perfect and obedient at all times and, for the love of God, don't touch her trinkets lying around her house.

Now those trinkets are mine.

And I can touch them whenever I damn well please.

Sometimes I do... just because I can. I'm an adult that way.

Silas comes to the door when we pull up. He doesn't look happy.

Then again, if I counted back to the night my mom died and forward, I can probably count on one hand how many days Silas really looked happy. He changed and definitely not for the better.

He's standing there in a dark gray suit, white shirt, and black tie. His dark brown hair is spiked a little in the front, but not enough to make him not look like a business asshole. His eyes are green. His beard has some red in it. He's as handsome as ever.

Why did I ever date him?

"You brought *him*." He doesn't say *him* with kindness.

"He was with me when you wouldn't stop texting. He was curious what you found."

"Yeah... I'm curious." I look behind me, and Abel is there. He's standing straight with his chest puffed out, reminding me of a gorilla getting ready to fight.

Okay then.

"This video doesn't concern you." Silas doesn't raise his voice. Silas, in my opinion, doesn't feel the need to raise it. He knows his shit doesn't stink, so why would he get irritated?

"It happened in my house. It attacked my mother. Killed my father and my sister. If you caught it on camera, then it damn well does concern me."

Silas seems to mull all that over. He takes me by the arm—not too forcefully, but enough where I can feel it—and whispers into my ear. "You don't want him seeing this footage. Trust me."

I almost laugh. Trusting Silas Ford isn't something I really want to do. It doesn't come naturally for me. It used to. Last year at this time, I would've said that my favorite activity was running into Silas's arms, going on a date with Silas, kissing Silas.

Why did it have to change?

"You want me... to trust you?" I try my hardest not to laugh. It wouldn't be nice to laugh. Course, since the concussion, I've done a lot of things that aren't too nice.

"You should on this." He gives me that I-mean-what-I-say look.

Abel seems to get the same vibe. "I'm watching it. End of story." He walks right by us and into my grandma's house.

Okay then. I guess we're doing this.

"Don't say I didn't warn you." Silas breathes into my ear. He turns on a dime. With his hands in his pockets, he's whistling Dixie as he disappears into the house.

Even though I'm the only person who is even supposed to be in the house by law, I stand outside. I don't know if I want to see the tapes now. I'm pretty sure I don't. If there's something on there Silas wants me to see but not Abel, it can't be good. Normally, I don't see Silas having a problem with it. I mean, it did happen in Abel's house. Why can't he see it? And why doesn't Silas want me to let Abel see it. He's his own man after all.

"Come on. Time is money." Silas calls out of the screen door. He disappears back into the house, and I take a deep breath.

A little heads-up of whatever this might be would be nice. Right now, it seems like it's very disjointed. If I know Silas, he's trying to manipulate me. Many have tried. Many have failed.

Curiosity gets the best of me, though. The familiar screen door squeak welcomes me to my grandma's. Immediately, I see my mom next to the stairs. She looks upset.

That makes two of us.

CHAPTER TWENTY-SIX

I WALK RIGHT PAST MY MOM. She won't say anything to me anyway. I look around for Abel's mom too. I'll tell him if I see her this time. I don't.

I join Silas and Abel in the living room. It's exactly how I left it. A large grandfather clock and a new television sitting on top of an old box one. Yup. Home sweet home.

Silas is messing with the television, trying to get it to play the videotape. "Does anyone still use video anymore?"

Silas doesn't pay me any never mind. "Elise, would I be trying to play a video if they didn't?"

"With you, who knows?" I wink at Abel. He doesn't wink back. He doesn't seem to be in the winking mood.

Okay then. I sit down on my couch in the same spot where I had my popcorn a few days ago, watching this the first time. This time, no popcorn. No easygoing banter between me and the television. With Abel here, this all seems way too real. Not that it didn't seem real the first time, but I wish I could've seen the video without Abel here with me. I mean, I don't mind it, and I do think he needs to know what's on it. But there is that unknown. What will be on the tape?

Will it upset Abel? Why didn't Silas want Abel to see it? No, he said that *I* wouldn't want Abel to see it.

I close my eyes. Can I please just take a nap? I did my good deed for the day.

Abel doesn't sit. He stands next to me with his arms crossed and his posture stiff. He's had a rough night too, and now this. I feel the same way. The exact same way.

Silas gets everything fixed and turns toward us. He looks at Abel and then directly at me. "Are you sure you want him in here to see this?"

"For the thousandth time, yes. He needs to see it. It's his family."

I glance up in enough time to see Abel give Silas the ha-ha glare. Silas, who I've never seen back down, backs down. "Okay, if you're sure."

Silas sits down on the coffee table but leaves enough room so I can see. He pushes fast forward on the video, and next to me, I see Abel flinch.

There is his family in all their glory. Breathing. Healthy. Alive.

These were their last moments on Earth, and we are about to re-watch it. Maybe once in his miserable life, Silas Ford was right. Maybe I shouldn't have let Abel stay. Then again, I'd hate to be the person to tell Abel he couldn't do anything. Silas is big, but Abel is bigger.

Silas stops it when they get to the interview right before the ghost comes in. "Now," Silas says. I can tell he's going to be like the annoying girl on the airplane telling you where all the exits are. "This is right before it all went down. Abel, I'm warning you. You might not want to watch this. It's unedited tape. Meaning this isn't the one that aired on the live network stream. We had another camera rolling. One I hooked up personally because I had a feeling about this house. It seemed... I don't know... off since I walked in."

"You having feelings now?" I try to go for the burn. I fail

miserably.

"I've always had feelings. I've always been good at my job, and it would've been really nice for someone to respect me for that."

I'm so glad Abel can witness our ex's spat. We are classy folks.

"Just get on with it," Abel says.

I can't imagine what's going through his mind right now. I mean, it's been a little more than a week since Halloween night, since he was in the same room where his family was killed. And now this?

I look up at him. He looks down at me. "I need to know," he whispers.

I know he does. I feel the same way about my mother. But I don't know if I want to see this now.

What are the options? That my father did it? That he was possessed? That someone else did it? That it really was the ghost anyway?

I take a deep breath as Silas finds the place he's looking for.

Abel, his mom, his dad, and his little sister walk into the room with the video equipment. They tell his sister not to touch anything. She really was a cute thing.

I glance up at Abel. His eyes are red, but no tears have fallen yet. They will, though. They always do. Despite what I say, you can't keep feelings locked away forever.

Abel's family is on the left. My dad and Silas are on the right. The kitchen is behind my dad and Silas. There is the hallway behind the Hales.

"Is there sound?" I ask.

Silas shakes his head. "Of course there's sound."

"That's convenient," Abel says.

"Just watch," Silas says. He's standing with the remote in his hand and his other hand on his chin. Thoughtful expression up in here.

The Hale family comes in and sits down. My dad and Silas sit across from them. They have decided to have a meeting where they can talk and try to get the spirit to communicate back. Seeing how this all ended, I bet they wish they hadn't done it.

Everything is the same as was on the live feed that I saw on the network, so far.

There were some words exchanged.

The lights flickered.

Then in a break in the static, I see it.

I see her.

Abel's sister points and screams.

Abel's mom scoots back and grabs Abel's arm. "You aren't taking him!" she yells.

Silas pauses the video.

"Oh my God." Abel sinks down to his knees on the floor. I'd do the same if I weren't already sitting on the couch.

There on the television screen, big as day, is the mass.

On this video, though, it isn't just a mass.

It's me.

"Care to explain that?" Silas says as he tosses the remote in the air and catches it. He's just in a big jolly mood.

It can't be me. There's no way. "I was here. I was at home. I mean here. I was eating popcorn and watching the live feed."

"Any proof of that?" Silas is actually questioning me on this.

"I don't need proof; it's the truth."

"Video doesn't lie." Why is he being such a butthole about this?

"You don't think... I was here. I was... I called Dad. Check his phone records. I called him to warn him."

"Warn him about what?" Silas asks. Like he doesn't know.

"About the black mass! I saw it."

"You... saw it." God he doesn't believe me. Why should

he? On the video there isn't a black mass. There's just me.

I'm smiling at the camera.

My eyes are black.

"That's not me." I'm as certain about this as I have been about anything in my life. That's not me. There's no way that's me. I was here."

"Again, do you have proof of that?" Silas raises an eyebrow.

I have nothing to say. Yes, I have proof. My dead mother's ghost saw me.

"Exactly. Look, I believe you, Elise."

"You never used to call me Elise. When did you start that?" Eli, he always called me Eli until my mom died and things went stupid.

"Elise is your name." Well that's simple. Elise was my name then too. It was my name on the night he took me back to his apartment, when I wanted him so bad I could taste it. He sent me home and told me it wasn't right. The next night, my mom died. I miss the old Silas.

"And no you don't believe me."

He sighs. "Yes, I do. I believe you, but don't think that means that others won't. That's you on this tape."

"Or something that looks like her." Abel chimes in for the first time. He's sitting on the edge of my grandma's couch. He's biting the side of his thumb. I guess he's trying to figure all of this out. Give some sort of explanation that makes sense.

"This was your plan?" Abel gripes, barely audible.

"What, like a twin?" Silas says incredulously, ignoring Abel.

"Like a something." Abel looks lost in thought, staring at the *me* on television with black eyes.

"Well, I live in the real world, children. I know if the police see this, they will arrest you, Elise, without question. It won't be your father who goes to jail for Abel's family's murder. It'll be you."

I stare at him, my mind swimming with thoughts. I can't concentrate on any of them. Does he really think it was me? Is he blackmailing me? What does Abel think about all of this? Surely, he doesn't think that's me on the video. It wasn't… it's not.

The *me* on TV winks.

"Whoa." Abel stands and points. "Did you see that?"

"I saw nothing." Silas turns off the television quickly and ejects the videotape. "But the police will."

"What do you want?" I suck in a breath and look Silas dead in the eyes. He won't get the best of me. I won't let him know that inside I'm a fragile and frazzled mess. He won't know. He can never know.

I won't let him.

"Want?" His dark eyes narrow as he places the videotape back into its case. "I'm sorry, I don't understand the question."

I can't believe I ever let that man touch me, much less kiss me. I can't even believe I had the thought of giving myself to him—he would've been my first. I'm a moron. "Yes, Silas, what do you want to keep that obviously doctored disk from the police?"

Silas smiles and taps the videotape against his palm. "You see, that's the interesting part. This video wasn't altered. It wasn't doctored. Believe me, I've run it through every program we have. It's honest to goodness what the camera caught that night."

A cold chill spreads down my spine, and I hug myself tightly. "I don't believe you. I was here. I know I was here. I saw a mass on the television. I called my dad." I can feel the tears, scared, frazzled tears, sting my eyes.

"I tried to warn him *and you*. I wasn't there. That's not me." I look at Abel. "I didn't kill your family. I promise."

I wish I could read his mind. I imagine he's as confused as I am. He's wanted evidence of what killed his family, and now he has it. And that evidence leads to me.

Oh God.

He'll hate me.

If he didn't hate me before, he'll hate me now.

"I know." His voice breaks, but he looks directly into my eyes. "I know you didn't." His words are barely above a whisper. I hope he truly believes that.

"This is a fun, morbid threesome we've got going on, but I have to say your secret's safe with me." Silas tosses me the videotape.

I catch it solid. No fumbling, even though my hands are shaking. "Why are you giving me this? Why wouldn't you go to the police?"

He puts his hands in his pockets and strolls passed Abel and toward the door. "Insurance."

"Insurance?"

"Oh, I have lots of copies of that videotape. So many I could send to the police, the FBI, TMZ, Oprah..."

"You son of a..." I march toward him, but Abel holds me back. "You'd really pin this on me. You know I didn't do it. You know it!"

"Video doesn't lie." He tilts his head. "Now does it? The police will see that tape and boom, little Elise Morgan will be in jail, and no one will believe it's a ghost. Because ghosts don't exist."

"You know they do." I seethe. He's seen too much stuff to say that to me.

"I know that, and you know that, and I assume Junior here knows that too. But let me tell you one thing I know for absolute fact: No matter what you say, according to anyone who matters, you were at the Hale house on Halloween. And you killed his family."

He's not wrong, and I hate it. I doubt I can reach the part of him that actually used to be nice. "Like I said five minutes ago, what do you want?"

"Like I said in that text... it seems like days ago now. The network is still interested in the show."

No. "And?"

"And, they want to revamp it. The public is pretty much salivating for some more *Dark and Deadly Things*. I don't get it either, but you know…"

I cross my arms. "And let me guess. You want me to sign over my dad's rights so you can be the sole star, right? I don't even think I can… I don't know…"

He holds up his hand to stop me. "Such a closed-minded little simpleton." He sighs and rubs his eyes like I've offended him with my stupidity. "I don't want the show. In fact, I won't even be on it. But you will… you and your little friend." His gaze moves slowly toward Abel.

There's no way Abel will do anything with me, much less go on television and hunt for ghosts.

"I'm listening," he says. His arm brushes up against my shoulder.

Silas smiles. "I knew you'd be on board."

Abel flinches.

"Stop gloating and tell me the plan." Abel ain't taking no shit from nobody right now. I like it.

"The plan is for *Dark and Deadly Things* to go in a different direction. Production crews are a lot of money, and they get in the way, as you recall."

I do recall. I never liked having a cameraman and sound guy behind me when I was investigating. And now they are both dead.

"The network has decided they want a documentary type show. Not a fake documentary show, but a real documentary show. You… with a camera. And Abel Hale… with a camera. That's it. No crew. No script. Just you." Silas sniffs like he's a rich son of a bitch. "I'll, of course, be the executive producer."

"All the money, none of the work." I scoff.

"All the money, none of the jail time," he says, pointing to the videotape wrapped up in my hands.

There are so many things wrong with this. Where will we get the cases? Why would anyone want us in their house? Where is the contract negotiation?

"We're in." Abel's lip twitches.

"Wait…"

"That's the right decision." Silas smiles and claps his hands together. "You won't regret it."

I already do.

"And just think, maybe, just maybe, in one of your investigations, you find the real thing that killed your family." Silas blinks a few times as he stands in the shadows by the door. "Wouldn't that be amazing?"

CHAPTER TWENTY-SEVEN

I FINISH LOCKING UP THE HOUSE and make my way toward Abel.

He's leaning on his car, his hands are in his pockets, and he's staring out toward town like he's got the weight of the world on his shoulders. I feel like I do too.

When I get to him, I mimic his posture and put my hands in my pockets. Damn, the hood of his car is cold. When did it get cold? "You don't have to do this, you know?"

"Yes I do." Short. Simple. Not so sweet.

"No, you don't. Silas blackmailing me doesn't have anything to do with you."

He doesn't smile. I was hoping he'd smile. "It has everything to do with me."

My phone vibrates in my pocket. When I look, sure enough, I see it's from Silas.

"Your boyfriend?" Abel doesn't look at me. I wonder if he'll ever look at me again.

"He's not my boyfriend."

"Yeah, I can't imagine you with him. He's lovely." Sarcasm. I love it.

"He used to be." I check my messages. "Not so much now."

"Got what he wanted and then left?"

I'm too busy reading the text to answer him right away. "Wait… what?"

"Never mind. Not important."

Did he seriously just ask if Silas and I had sex?

"What does it say?" Abel asks, totally changing the subject. I appreciate that.

"My dearest ELI, come by my office tomorrow and we'll sign the contracts. Your first case is in Millersville, Kentucky. It is about a five-hour drive. You're expected on Friday. When you come to sign your contracts, I'll have your cameras for you. You'll both be paid only if you find evidence at each location. Good luck… and you made the right decision."

I turn the phone off and fight every urge I have to throw it on the ground. "I guess we're heading to Millersville." Abel sighs.

"No, I'm going to Millersville. Me. I'm the one he's blackmailing. You're free to do whatever you want."

He turns toward me, his eyes dark. "Do you know what I want, Elise? I want to go home. I want to kiss my mom and dad. I want to be mad at my little sister. But I can't do anything like that. So, you may think that this is all about you, and I'm just here to keep you from getting in trouble with the police. But I'm not. I have my own reasons for going on this hunt, which have nothing to do with you and are truly none of your business."

I start to say it wasn't me. He stops me mid-thought. "I know it isn't your fault. I know that. But I also know I can't explain that tape, and I can't explain what happened in my house, what had been happening up until then. I don't know who or what this Molly is that my sister talked about, or if she even is a somebody. I don't know why my mom grabbed my arm to protect me from it. But I do know if I can help someone else, like we saved Julie's family, then I want to do it. I have to do it. And if I can find the thing that killed my family… then that's a bonus."

Tears sting my eyes. "What if that thing turns out to be me?"

I wait an eternity for his answer. No matter what I said, there is still a very small part deep inside that is terrified the thing on the screen was somehow me. I'm terrified of myself. I'm terrified Abel will leave me, and I'll be all alone. The longer he waits to answer, the more that fear grows.

"Then it's a good thing you are with me. Makes hunting you down much easier."

Without a smile, a smirk, a hint of *I'm kidding* in his voice, Abel turns his back toward me and gets into the driver's side. That's it. That's all he has to say about it.

I wipe the tears from my eyes. They won't do any good anyway.

Abel starts up the engine, making me jump from the hood. I don't have anything else I can do. My family has been destroyed. My ex-boyfriend is setting me up, and my new friend may or may not trust me—I vote for *may not*.

With my head down, I slide my feet across the pavement until I reach his passenger's door. I guess this is it for us. For the near future, it's me and Abel. Abel and me.

I shut the door, and he pulls away from my grandma's home. He stops at my dorm long enough for me to pick up some clothes. I tell Naked Girl goodbye, and that I'd see her soon. When I get back, I'll try the EVP app on her. I promise her again.

She shoots me a bird and glitches away.

Abel stays in the car and only gets out when the time comes to load the trunk.

I don't take much. It's just a weekend trip to Millersville, right?

We'll be back soon.

I try not to think about the one thing that won't leave me alone.

Abel's family is dead. Mine is gone.

And that figure on the videotape looks exactly like me. Like, exactly.

Except her eyes, dark-as-night eyes.

I don't know what she was, but I have my theories. I hope to God I'm wrong.

We speed down the road in silence.

Abel is my constant for now.

I lean back and shut my eyes.

The *me* on the television's black eyes stare back at me.

DARK AND DEVIOUS THINGS
Book 2
February 2017

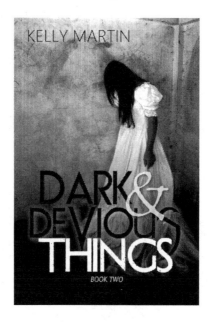

Find out more at
www.kellymartinbooks.com

Giveaways, contests, and news before anyone else
Newsletter: http://bit.ly/KellyMartinSignup

Find Kelly Martin online:
Facebook: KellyMartinAuthor
Youtube: youtube.com/c/KellyMartinBooks
Twitter: @martiekay
Instagram: kellymartin215
Pinterest: KMBooks

OTHER BOOKS BY KELLY MARTIN

Paranormal

The Afterlife of Lizzie Monroe

The Heartless Series

Heartless

Soulless

Breathless

Reckless

Hart

Historical

Fairy Tale Series

Betraying Ever After

The Beast of Ravenston

The Glass Coffin

Contemporary

The Deception of Devin Miller

BIG is Beautiful: A Love Story

Mystery

Hindsight Series:

Out of the Blue

The Black Heart

Red Scarlet

YA Inspirational

Crossing the Deep

Saint Sloan

Saving Sloan

Sacrificing Sloan

Love in the 80s

Once Bitten, Twice Shy

Made in the USA
San Bernardino, CA
25 August 2017